Sky Hunter

The Targon Tales

Chris Reher

Chris Reher

The Targon Tales

Sky Hunter

The Catalyst

Only Human

Rebel Alliances

Delphi Promised

Quantum Tangle

Terminus Shift

Entropy's End

also available in eBook and audio format

www.chrisreher.com

All rights reserved.
ISBN: 978-0-9921090-1-1
Copyright © 2013 Chris Reher

Thank You, as always,

to Tracy Leach and Dee Solberg

Chris Reher

ONE

The sight of nine Air Command Kites swooping around the towering buttes guarding the plains of Bellac Tau was either a thing of beauty or of terror, depending on whose side of the war observed the approach. The planes arrived, cloaked by technology as much as the dawn, to deliver their payload only hours after leaving the Union's military base on the other side of the flatlands.

"Downtown is in sight," Nova Whiteside said when the external cameras confirmed what her onboard navigator had found.

"But where is everybody?" her wingman's voice came from the speakers in her helmet. "I thought this was going to be fun."

The dusty settlement supposedly making a living by catering to the tribes of nomadic locals huddled empty and desolate in the lee of the foothills. They knew enough about this continent to expect open markets, animal pens, caravans and desert vehicles among the brick buildings. None of that in sight, nobody home. Something had compelled the plains people to heed their ancient instincts for self-preservation and move on to some other village.

"Going to have to poke a stick in it," she said.

A scattering of metal sheds, much newer than the town, came into view and into her gun sights. They housed Rhuwacs, according to the scouts, barely-sentient creatures trained by the Shri-Lan rebels to invade towns and villages, maiming and destroying as directed by their handlers. Cheap, expendable, and easily-replaced cannon fodder imported to this remote planet for just that purpose.

"Chow time! I think someone's noticed us now."

Nova's sensors showed a horde of them pouring out of the buildings when the attacking Air Command squad pounced onto the village. She did not zoom in for a closer look, knowing these people to be slow-moving mountains of muscle under skin so thick that it often cracked in places to give the appearance of scales. Armed with cudgels, simple ballistic weapons, knives and massive teeth, they stood little chance against the airborne threat descending upon them. This was the third of such camps found and routed along the Rim.

"Whiteside, Tonda," her flight lead's voice reached her. "Check out the cave system Jack found before they scram. We'll clean out the Rhuwacs."

"Aye. Save me some, will you?" Nova replied and veered east, toward the coordinates provided by their scouts.

"Just get that bunker, Lieutenant."

"Bunker, right," she mumbled to herself. "Now where did they put that bunker?" The plane faithfully obeyed her mental commands, conveyed via the neural interface at her temple, to navigate while she consulted the sensors. They knew the location precisely and finding it was not the problem.

"Probably shielded," Tonda said. His plane glided noiselessly beside her own Kite toward the sporadically forested hills edging the salt flats. "They know we're coming."

A steady ticking sound over their receivers indicated that someone had tapped into their communication. "I don't know how Dakad expects us to find it up here," she said to those who might be listening. "No one mentioned all those tree-things." She turned her head and signaled to Tonda through her cockpit canopy. He veered away.

She swung the other way, her mind now entirely on directing the Kite toward the next valley where the rebels had hidden their important goodies below ground. Com arrays, weapons, senior members of the faction, likely valuables and contraband as well. The town they had left at the edge of the plains was as expendable as the Rhuwacs corralled there.

Shooting at a pack of mishandled Rhuwacs was a favorite bloodsport among her fellow soldiers and pilots but Nova was secretly glad not to have a part of that today. The creatures, although without empathy and trained to kill, were not animals and their role as enemy simply a matter of relentless and cruel conditioning. The Union's xenologists had classified them as sentient, a Prime species, and none of this was of their making.

Worse yet, the ramshackle town that her squad was about to destroy surely also housed civilians, even if most of them seemed to have deserted it. A discouraging number of the red-skinned, white-haired Bellac natives had sided with the rebels, but most of the residents of this remote region cared nothing about either the Commonwealth of United Planets or the rebel factions that opposed it. She hoped that the presence of the Rhuwacs had driven the locals from the valley.

Nova shook herself out of these thoughts. "Blow stuff up, Nova," she said. "Get back home in one piece. That's it, that's all."

"Huh?" came Tonda's startled reply.

"Going over my notes," she said. She saw him approaching from the east now to rendezvous above the coordinates they had been given. At this distance, his Kite looked like a dark, graceful bird swooping over the treetops. Deploying the ordnance designed to penetrate shielding known to be used by rebels was not, unlike some of their other weaponry, a long-distance maneuver. "Do we have news?" she asked, both of him and her own systems in search of the shield's configuration.

"Yep," he said and she could almost see the grin on the Centauri's face. "Calibrating now."

"Clever, clever rebels," Nova said when her sensors picked up the communications array embedded in the bare face of a cliff, invisible from afar. The entrance to the bunker would be at the foot of that rock, behind a line of trees. In this part of the planet the trees were little more than gaunt frames for long ropes of gray-green foliage but still dense enough to impede a clear vision of the ground. "Fire at will," she said.

Instead of seeing tracers issue from his Kite, a much broader trail shot up from the ground just as her system warned of additional power sources below them. "Abort," she shouted. "Shielded anti-aircraft positions. We're too low. Abort!" She broke to the right, away from the valley, expecting Tonda to do likewise. "Whiteside to Dakad." She switched her com system to reach her wing commander. "Taking fire from the ground. Looks like coilers. Requesting backup."

The reply was a curse.

"Yessir," she said. "Four launches."

"Manage, Whiteside," Captain Dakad snarled. "We're taking fire, too. Someone knew we were coming long before we left the damn base."

"Three now," Tonda corrected. "Got one gone. Where the hell did they get those? What kind of lunatic uses coilers on the ground? Jack didn't mention any of this. Remind me to kick his buttery ass when I—"

"Tonda!" Nova shouted when she saw the other Kite spin away. "Captain, he's taken fire." She veered to describe a wide arc around the likely range of the gun on the ground. Her weapons training did not include anticipating armament not even meant to work inside an atmosphere such as Bellac's. When she saw the telltale tracer of another missile race toward her she rolled and returned fire. The explosion below her confirmed the hit.

"Going down," Tonda yelled, his words distorted by

panic. He was barely twenty-five, by Human terms, and this tour was his first aboard a Kite. "Got holed, elevators toasted. I can't punch out!"

Nova watched him streak away from the valley in search of a place to land. She came about when her scanner reported another launch from the ground. The guns had an impressive reach but not enough speed for the Kite's evasive maneuvers. She eluded that one as well and blanketed the location with a few missiles of her own. "Tonda! Did you bail? Tell me you made it."

"Made it. Sort of," he groaned. "Kite's down and not in a good way. From what I can see through all the blood on the dash."

Nova cursed and set after him. She found him in a clearing left by a long-ago rock slide. His Kite leaned drunkenly among some boulders but seemed largely intact. She hovered overhead. "Captain, Kite Four is down. Tonda's still in it. Still talking."

"Where?"

"Too close. If they have skimmers they'll be here in minutes." She scanned the area around the downed plane. To allow even a damaged Kite to fall into enemy hands was unthinkable.

There was a brief silence. "Mitigate."

"By *Cazun*!" Tonda's oath was a mere whimper.

"Sir?"

"Deal with it, Whiteside!" Dakad shouted.

Nova circled the wreck, knowing damn well that she was pointing out their location to anyone looking skyward even if their own scanners hadn't shown them yet. Mitigate. Meaning, don't leave the rebel with anything valuable. Not a plane and not a hostage. She glanced over her available arsenal.

"Gods, Nova," Tonda said as if he could see her finger on the trigger.

She ground her teeth. "I'm not leaving you." She took manual control over from her neural interface, expecting the

Kite to refuse to land here. Indeed, her warning systems engaged peevishly while the vertical descent system hovered her Kite lower, into a clear space not far from Tonda's plane. The camera at the belly of her plane found a few spots for the landing struts to settle among the rocks. She exhaled sharply. "Can you make it here, Tonda?"

"No. I'm stuck."

She switched the Kite's sensor output to the data sleeve on her forearm. Snatching up a gun, she climbed out of the cockpit and slid over the edge of the triangular wing onto the rocky ground. The loose scree sliding out from under her boots slowed her sprint to Tonda's plane. A glance to her screen showed four vehicles approaching from her left, just above treetop elevation. "That's what I get for saying 'skimmer' out loud," she said to herself.

She climbed up to his cockpit canopy, already shattered by his attempt to eject. The missile had impacted somewhere below the pilot seat and warped pieces of the interior had cut deep into Tonda's leg and right arm. "Damn," Nova breathed when she saw the damage, again grudgingly impressed by the rebels' ability to innovate. She leaned heavily against a piece of the starboard console that had wedged across Tonda's knees, hoping that the ejectors didn't choose this moment to deploy. "You Centauri are just too long for these seats. Move!"

He heaved himself past her, out of the cockpit and onto the wing. With a groan, he let himself slide to the ground where he collapsed. She followed after entering a command code that would destroy the plane's onboard programs and data storage. "Get up, they're coming." She grasped his parachute harness to pull him up again. His face was about as pale as a Centauri could get and the violet eyes had turned nearly gray. "Stay with me now," she snapped.

They stumbled back to her plane where she pushed him up into the cockpit to crumple into the small space behind the pilot seat. The shock of his injuries had worn off and he howled in pain. Nova leaped into her seat and launched at once, somewhat unsteadily because of the terrain and the extra weight behind her but the Kite finally agreed to cooperate. She rose up and shot away from the wreck.

"What are you doing?" Tonda exclaimed.

She moved out of coiler range and focused on the plane's sensors. "Did you nick an artery or something urgent?"

"What? No."

"Then shut up a moment," she said. "Don't bleed on stuff." She swung around in a wide circle, waiting, counting. The four skimmers had arrived at the downed plane now. Three more were closing in from the direction of the bunker. When they had all stopped she turned the Kite and raced back to the site. Wasting no time with a close approach, she lobbed an incendiary missile at the wreck which promptly exploded in spectacular fashion, disintegrating the skimmers and whatever number of rebels they had brought with them.

"Holy shit!" Tonda's voice was a high-pitched squeal. He peered at the inferno below them as the mossy trees caught fire, fully aware that, if not for her abstract interpretation of Dakad's orders, he would have gone up along with them.

Nova did not reply. She brought the plane around and headed for the coordinates of the bunker. There was one more gun out here somewhere but she hoped that everyone was too busy thinking about what had just happened to look up at the silent Kite over their heads. She unloaded her entire arsenal at the bunker entrance and watched the side of the cliff collapse onto the tunnels below before breaking away to rejoin their squadron.

It was only when they had cleared the badlands and saw the plains before them that she noticed her hands shaking on the control panel. "I might puke," she said.

"Whiteside," Tonda grunted through clenched teeth. "If my bits are still where I last saw them, will you have my babies?"

She laughed, aware of the note of hysteria that accompanied it but needing to laugh anyway, whooping with glee to burn off the overwhelming adrenaline that still surged through her body. Gradually, her heart rate returned to normal, at least according to the Kite's sensors, and she was able to breathe evenly again.

They soon reached the devastated rebel compound where the battle had ended not long ago. She circled for a moment to look over a field strewn with building and machine parts, Rhuwac bodies and, sadly, a large scorch mark where another of the expensive Kites had met its end. Nothing moved down there although her sensors showed life forms not far from the perimeter. Escaped rebels, perhaps, or just Bellac scavengers. "I think I'm in trouble," she said.

"Damn right you are," a harsh voice cut across the com link. "Get your ass back to the base."

An hour or two later Nova did just that. She had stopped only briefly atop one of the mesas scattered over the plains to patch Tonda up as best as she could with the basic kit available to them. The rest of her squad had slowed to let her catch up and no one spoke until they reached the installation.

Rim Station served as a temporary sentinel at the edge of the great equatorial plains of Bellac Tau, far removed from anything even remotely civilized. It dispatched airborne patrols to rout rebel hideouts along the edges of the barren expanse of scrubland, and two units of ground combat troops provided security for the handful of towns nestled in the surrounding hills. Most of those stationed here assumed that the word 'temporary' had been tagged on to excuse its neglected state of windblown shabbiness. That there was no end to the need to control rebel incursions was made clear every day.

A trolley dispatched by the base clinic was waiting when she touched down and she loitered while Tonda was loaded into it, hoping to avoid her squadron leader for a few more minutes.

Tonda reached out to tug on her sleeve. "Whiteside, if you get field boarded I'll come visit you in lockup. I'll bring candy."

"Just glad you're still with us, Tonda. Get gooder soon."

"Are you injured, Lieutenant?" a medic asked her. He patted her face with a cloth that smelled of disinfectant.

"No, it's all his," she said and allowed him to wipe the streaks of blood from her face and hands. Her flight suit, too, was smeared with it but there was nothing to be done about that now. Quickly, she shook her hair out and retied the unruly red strands without the benefit of a mirror.

Once Tonda was carted away she nodded to the mechanics to go ahead and tow her Kite to the hangars where someone would have to remove a whole lot of blood from the rear compartment. When it moved out of the way she saw Captain Dakad waiting for her. For a giddy moment she imagined that it was the glower on his face, not the heat of the day, that made the air shimmer between them. He disappeared into the outbuilding that served them as a ready room at the edge of the airfield.

The debrief had already begun when she arrived there. Dakad paused for an instant before returning his attention to the display screens. She walked to the back, briefly tapping the raised hand of one of the other pilots as she passed. She was a little surprised when the man beside him, Lieutenant Heiko Boker, moved over to make room for her. As the only female pilot on this remote outpost, acceptance among them had been a struggle since arriving here weeks ago.

"You got the stones, Whiteside," he whispered without looking at her.

She hid a smile when she dropped into the seat beside him.

The debrief moved on with detailed accounts of numbers and casualties, speculations about the unusual weapon in rebel hands, maneuvers carried out and targets missed. Their planes' video and sound recordings were studied in detail. She winced when she heard that Lieutenant Avlin, a friendly and well-liked wing mate, was the one whose plane was downed by the surprising defense staged by the Shri-Lan rebels. At length, Dakad's eyes found her in the back of the room.

"Perhaps Lieutenant Whiteside will offer some insights into her decision-making abilities today."

Nova stood up to face their squadron leader, a rangy Centauri whose long and undistinguished career had shifted him from one front line tour to the next. "Sir, there was time to retrieve Lieutenant Tonda. So I did."

"Were those your orders?"

"Not precisely, sir." She squared her shoulders. "You ordered mitigation. I mitigated. It worked." Boker, beside her, exhaled audibly and sunk lower in his seat.

"So it did," Dakad said. His violet eyes moved over the other pilots. "By risking another pilot and another plane in deciding to land a Kite on unknown terrain in rebel-held territory for which you knew we had faulty intel. Is that your idea of mitigation?"

"As I said, there was enough time before the skimmers reached the site. My intent, until I saw the damage, was to switch planes with Lieutenant Tonda."

"Really," the captain said. "And why is that? Because you're so much better a pilot than he is?"

She frowned. All of them knew that she was the better pilot. "Well, yes. Sir." She recognized a dangerous twitch in his eye but continued. "And he was injured, sir. It seemed a good idea at the time."

"A good idea is for you to stick to SOP."

"Yessir."

"Why are we here, Whiteside?"

"On Bellac, sir?"

"Are you someplace else?"

Nova felt herself begin to sweat, wondering what point the captain had to make in front of her squad. "No, sir." She glanced at the other pilots. "Air Command's mission on Bellac Tau is to remove the Shri-Lan rebels from the Rim towns and provide security while the elevator to the new orbiter is constructed."

"And why do we give a damn about a bunch of cattle herders on the other end of this godforsaken desert?"

"We need Bellac Tau to join the Union," she began by rote. "The new jumpsite we just mapped will cut interstellar travel to Magra by half but it's situated inside Bellac air space. Taking stewardship of the site will let us control rebel activity in this sub-sector. Bellac won't let us post a manned relay near the gate until the rebel is neutralized on the surface and the skyranch is complete."

Dakad nodded. "And what problem do we have here, Whiteside?"

She suppressed a sigh. "We're shorthanded, under-equipped, under-supplied and outnumbered by Rhuwacs," she said, echoing a complaint he voiced at every opportunity but leaving out the expletives that usually accompanied it.

He raised his arms and addressed the rest of the group. "And so you decide to be a hero and gamble another pilot and another plane because you think you know how long it takes to extract an injured pilot from a crash site."

"Given the option..." she began.

"Yes, Whiteside? What were the options?"

She winced. "Mitigation. Destroying the plane on the ground. With Tonda in it."

"Which you refused to consider."

"You told me to handle it," she said, irritated now. "So I did."

"By risking your life and plane over a rookie pilot. A greenie," he added, referring to the green uniforms issued at the flight academies. His eyes narrowed. "Because you don't have the nerve to make that call when it gets down to it."

She took a deep breath, now only moments from losing her temper. Before she could voice her views on teamwork and duty to one's squadron she felt a tap on her foot. When she glanced down at Boker she saw him shake his head in a minute gesture. She remained silent.

"You're escorting the Yasser transport for the next five days," Dakad said. "Dismissed. All of you." He stomped from the shed without looking at any of them again.

Nova dropped into her seat with a groan and a curse

while the other six pilots slowly moved to the exit.

One of the Centauri, Lieutenant Sulean, turned back. "Thanks for getting him out, Whiteside," he said. "We'll go check on him."

She nodded and watched them leave. Their Caspian wingman shuffled by and slowed to tap her shoulder, as did Lieutenant Cee. Finally only Boker and the other Human, Rolyn, remained.

Boker turned to her. "You took that beating well, Whiteside," he said.

She closed her eyes for a moment. "What the hell was that about?"

"The man's an ass." He shrugged. "He's wrong and that's his way of making sure we get our story straight. He couldn't hold it together trying to run the scramble in town and manage you out there as well. You called in just after Avlin went down. Easier to just pull the plug on your problem. If you had actually followed procedure we'd be short one Tonda now and it would have been Dakad's fault for losing his wad."

She sat up. "Did he really expect me to give Tonda up just like that? Is that what you do here?"

He shook his head. "Any pilot worth his plane would have tried to extract Tonda. You did right. You had enough time but Dakad'll never admit it. But this isn't Targon or Magra or wherever you came from. Best to just shut up and let it happen. It's only a six month tour."

The pilots gathered up their gear and left the building. A hot breeze pushed dust across the tarmac and the sun glared red over the horizon, about to drop off the plateau on which the base was built. The ground crew, nearing the end of their shift, seemed less energetic now in preparing for the last of the returning squads.

"Do you think I'll have to hear more about this?" Nova asked.

"Nah," Rolyn said. "He doesn't want any attention on this or he'd have given you more than babysitting chores as punishment. But watch him take the credit for saving the pilot, if not the plane. By tonight what you did will be what he meant by 'mitigate' all along."

"And no mention made about the bunker you took out by yourself," Boker added.

"That flight better count!"

"Has to," Rolyn assured her. "We saw the video. How short are you now?"

Nova pretended to calculate the numbers she carried engraved in her heart and mind. "If I get proper credit for this sortie, I'll need sixty more hours to qualify."

Boker whistled. "Almost there, then. We'll have a bona fide Hunter Class pilot in our midst. Don't get hard to talk to."

"Well, that's just to qualify. I still have to get through the tests."

He waved his hands in a dismissive gesture that nearly caught Rolyn across the forehead. "Bah, can't be harder than pulling a greenie out of a downed plane on the side of a hill. Been a long day, Whiteside. How about you join me and Rolie for a bottle of the rotgut after chow?"

Nova smiled at the officer. This was the first time someone included her so casually in their downtime since she had arrived here. She felt like something had changed here today, finally. And if it meant taking a dressing down from the captain it had been worth it. But she had long ago decided to keep a careful distance between herself and the male pilots' after-hours entertainment. Unfortunately, other than a few mechanics and some base staff, there were few women here, none of them pilots, with whom she could share her free time. Something else she had to get used to out here, she supposed. "Thanks, but I think I'll go hug my pillow. If I have to shuttle to Yassar and back all day I'll need to stay awake." She waved and jumped onto a runabout heading to the hangars.

TWO

The smile still hadn't left Nova's face when the service cart turned toward an outbuildings, leaving her at the main hangar. Cutting through the repair bays would take her straight to the pilots' dorms before the others beat her to the decon facilities. A quick bite of whatever was to be found in the mess hall followed by a long sleep was the only thing on her mind now. Despite the captain's tirade, this had been a remarkable day, indeed.

The main work shift was winding down in the bays, too. No night flights were scheduled and the techs had put their tools away until the morning. Bellac's swift rotation made for short nights and all species used to longer rests tried to manage as much of that as possible.

She ducked through a row of planes waiting for their service and then scaled an elevated catwalk. The heavy tread of several pairs of boots on metal stairs made it clear that she was not the only one taking this shortcut. Ahead of her another catwalk met the one she was using and she saw a ground combat squad ambling toward her. The shadowless glare of the overhead lights revealed five Centauri and three Human soldiers, likely just now returning from one of the Rim towns for downtime. One of them grabbed another's arm as if to shove him over the low railing and into the repair pits below. The others laughed raucously when he pulled the smaller man back just in time, earning a barrage of insults involving his dubious parentage.

Nova smiled to herself but kept walking, hoping to reach the doors at the far end of the walkway before one of these louts decided to give her a fright, too. But she had most definitely used up her allotment of good luck for the day. The men reached the intersection before she did and there were a few elbow nudges when they discovered her walking toward them. Most of them nodded to her, the two sergeants among them saluted casually, and they kept walking.

All but three. Nova groaned inwardly when they stopped to wait for her approach. Base grunts, from the looks of them. Shaved heads, sweat-stained shirts and ill-used fatigues. Neckless blocks of muscle designed for close combat of which, judging by the mass of scars covering one of the soldiers' neck and arm, they had seen plenty.

"Lieutenant," the towering Centauri greeted her. The two Humans with him moved into the middle of the catwalk, blocking her way.

"Evening," she said with a glance over the railing. There was no one down there now. The other soldiers had neared the doors and did not look back. Nova continued her brisk pace as if the two Humans were not in her way. They had little choice but to step aside or risk colliding with her. As she passed, she felt a large hand on her rump, tightening to squeeze her almost painfully. She whirled around to glare at the man.

"You got a problem, soldier?"

He grinned and raised his hands in defense. "No harm intended. Just hard to pass up such a nice ass, is all. Not many of those around here."

She scowled at him. "Who's your CO?"

The men stared at her for a moment before laughing in unison. "Got a complaint, do you?" the Centauri said. "Complain about this." He grabbed her upper arm to draw her close but released it again when she pushed away from him.

"I don't think she likes you," his Human companion said.

"I don't think I like any of you," she said. "I don't suggest you try that again."

The easy grin on the Centauri's face disappeared. "Or what?" He gripped her arm again only to find her pistol jammed under his nose. He froze when he heard the quiet whine of the charge in the sudden silence.

"Don't be looking for trouble, girl," the scarred Lieutenant said after a stunned moment.

"Back," she said to the Centauri, who obeyed her command. "I am looking for dinner, not to entertain a bunch of Rhuwac-brained grunts."

A door below them screeched on its metal track and a supply cart trundled into the space. Nova took that moment to turn and rush toward the door into the main base, not quite willing to give the men the satisfaction of seeing her run, but not wasting any time reaching the more populated hallways beyond.

* * *

Finally! Nova thought when, an hour later, she returned to her small room. After a visit to the decon station for a clean-up and a hurried stop for dinner, she was ready to fall into her cot. Her quarters, like those of the other junior officers, offered little in the way of luxury or comfort but luckily, as the only female pilot on this small base, she had no roommate.

"Yes, yes, time for bed," she said to a picture of a grush cat someone had sketched for her after hearing that she had never owned a pet. An Air Command military base on one planet or another was all she had ever known and neither the lack of amenities nor pets had ever bothered her. An army brat from birth, the frugal soldier's accommodations were all the homey comforts she needed.

She slipped into a robe and took a few moments to comb her thick mane of copper hair, more than ready for sleep.

A knock on her door forced a tired groan from her lips. "I'm asleep. Go away!"

"It's Captain Beryl, Lieutenant. A word, please."

She frowned and went to the door to open it for the officer. "Is there an emergency, sir?" she asked, surprised when the man stepped into her room without invitation. He was not her commanding officer and his late-night visit was certainly out of the ordinary. She had seen him on the base many times; his primary function was to oversee the movement of ground troops between the home base and their various combat missions into the Rim towns. Like his men, he was a hulking, scarred tank, distinguishable from them only by his insignia.

He looked around the room before turning to her. "I hear you met some of my boys today," he said.

Her brow furrowed. "Yes, they were definitely behaving like boys. It's a shame, seeing how two of them were officers."

He nodded. "The ones you assaulted."

"What?" she gasped. Had she heard that wrong?

"You drew your gun on one of my men. What were you thinking?"

"Look, Captain," she said, feeling anger rise to where it would soon cause her to say something unbecoming an officer. She pointed at the door to show him out. "Take your grievances to my CO. It's late and this is not the time for this conversation. Or the place."

"Last time I checked I'm the one who says what it's time for," he said. "You pilots seem to think that rank and file doesn't matter out here. Well it does, Lieutenant. On this mission your fucking arrogance will get you killed. So stand at attention when addressing a superior."

Reluctantly, Nova complied.

"That's better," he said. "You're new here, Whiteside. You don't know how this base is run. Pissing off those men can be a very dangerous way to spend your time here."

Nova said nothing. Beryl wasn't here to get her side of

the story.

He turned in the small space and perched on the edge of her storage cabinet. "This place is hard on a man," he said. "Long deployments, hot weather, crap food, snipers, fucking rebels using every trick never taught in basic training."

She wondered if she was expected to sympathize with him at this point. He looked like he'd never had a comfortable tour of duty in his life. Why was he complaining to her?

"So the boys have to cut loose once in a while. You know there aren't a lot of women on the base. A man gets tired of the Bellac whores here. Getting your ass grabbed once in a while isn't exactly worth shooting people over."

"If you value discipline so much you should be instilling that into your men. I'm not here for their amusement."

"You don't get it, do you, Whiteside?" His eyes had settled on her chest and seemed content to stay there. "If you can't handle that sort of prank you should not have come here. You could have taken another assignment instead of front line. So now you're going to have to fit in."

"This is outrageous!" she hissed. "I'm an Air Command officer. Your men were out of line."

"I know," he said and rose to his full height. "I can make sure it doesn't happen again."

"Good," she said. "No apologies needed. Just tell them to stay out of my way."

He took a step closer to her. She flinched when he raised a massive hand to cup her chin. "They will stay away from you if they knew you were... under my personal protection."

She blinked, not sure if she understood what he was proposing. "What?"

His hand came to rest on her shoulder. "No one will touch you again as long as you show me a little appreciation for that."

Nova laughed harshly. "You're out of your mind. Get out of my room."

A terrible darkness moved over his already severe

features. Before she could react he tore her loosely tied robe open and reached around her to pin her arms behind her back. She gasped when he forced her bare chest to press against his. "Then how about I show you what you can expect from my boys," he growled.

She struggled to escape his grip, overwhelmed by his size and strength.

"Go ahead, yell. Digger's in the hallway. Just don't think he'll be rescuing you if he comes in here."

She snapped her head forward and sunk her teeth into the skin of his jaw.

He reeled back, releasing her to clutch his face, checking for blood. "Little bitch!" He grabbed her arm when she turned to run to the door. Nova suddenly found herself airborne when he flung her across the room, over her bunk, to careen into the wall. A sickening bolt of pain shot through her shoulder when she crashed to the floor.

Beryl lurched over her bunk to haul her up again. "Looks like you popped a joint there, Whiteside," he said and pushed her down onto the bed.

Nova struggled weakly, fighting an urge to either throw up or faint, aware of little more than the pain from her dislocated shoulder. She stared in disbelief when he reached down to unbuckle his fatigues. She had to get out of here, get away from this monster now clutching her legs.

"Could have done this friendly." The captain leaned over her when she tried to roll away. He pressed one hand over her mouth and the other onto the grotesque lump distending her shoulder. She screamed into his hand until, almost gratefully, she passed out.

* * *

She was alone now. Alone with pain that flared up the moment she stirred on her bed. She groaned loudly and then pinched her lips tight when, little by little, she shifted her body until she finally sat on the edge of her bed.

Nova looked around her room as if her assailant might

still be lurking in one of its corners. How long had she been unconscious?

She pushed herself off the bed and fought a wave of dizziness before she could see again. It seemed to take forever to pull on a pair of loose-fitting trousers and fasten her robe. Tears of pain and anger spilled over her face and she wiped at them away, annoyed with herself for falling into Beryl's trap. This wasn't the academy and this wasn't Targon. She had already seen enough here to realize the difference between the stringently ruled airfields where she had trained and worked and this backwater outpost. She had hoped to learn much during a tour under rougher conditions but this lesson was not one she had prepared for.

There was no one in the night-silent hall when she moved toward the stairs. The base clinic was a below the pilots' floor and she was glad when no one met her on the way down there. Her knees felt unsteady, her long hair was a tangle and her face a puffy mess. She was not surprised when a medic rushed toward her, looking alarmed, when she walked into the med center.

"What the hell happened to you?" he exclaimed.

She pulled back before he could take her arm. "Get Doctor Soren."

"She's asleep. Come in here." He put his hand on her back to guide her into an examination room.

"Touch me and I will break your nose," she growled.

The medic looked at her quizzically for a long moment before nodding. "I see. Wait here."

Nova sat on the edge of the exam table, cradling her useless arm and wondered how she had stooped from being hailed as a most promising junior officer among her peers to this. There was no part of her body that didn't ache and her mind continued to throw up images of Beryl's contorted face hovering above her. She stood up and paced, almost glad when her shoulder began to throb more excruciatingly to chase those images from her mind.

At last, the female medic arrived, obviously just pulled

from her bed to attend to Nova. She was still running her fingers through her tousled hair when she entered the room. Like many Bellacs, she used brilliant dyes to decorate the naturally white strands.

"Are you going to tell me who did this or will I wait for the DNA results to find out for myself?" she greeted Nova while she prepared a hefty dosage of painkiller.

"Captain Beryl," Nova said into the plastic cup held to her face. She inhaled deeply and soon felt the pain in her shoulder subsiding. A languid, rubbery feeling surged through her body and she suspected something more than painkiller in the dose she was receiving.

"Beryl himself, huh?" Soren began to manipulate Nova's arm. "This okay?"

"Yes, just do it," Nova said.

There was no sudden jolt, just some careful handling of her arm and then her shoulder joint slid back into its accustomed place. The remaining pain stopped nearly at once.

"Hold it like this. Better?" Soren asked, looking into Nova's ashen face. "Shall we take a look at the works?"

Nova nodded. "Are you going to report this to Major Trakkas right away?"

Soren tilted her head. "The post commander? Are you sure?"

"He's in charge of personnel. Who else would I complain to?"

"Someone who doesn't think Beryl is the star of the show around here."

Nova put her clothes on a nearby chair to submit to the exam. Bruises were inspected, samples were taken, wounds cleaned. Neither of them spoke during the procedure, giving Nova time to think about her request.

At last, Soren covered her patient with a thin sheet and sat on a stool beside the table on which she lay. She entered some information into the slim data tablet in her hands. "You're off duty for a few days. That shoulder is going to feel like a massacre tomorrow. I'll give you some tranks for it. You're also seeing the post-trauma folks first thing."

"Is that necessary?"

"It's what's best. You combat grunts might have had to prepare yourselves for the kind of horrors you encounter but it's policy. They're getting great results with cognitive processing."

Nova grimaced. "Messing around with your memories. No thanks. I like my head where it is."

"No one's going to do that. It just lets you re-associate what happened to make it more tolerable. I've seen them get some pretty horrific cases back on their feet fast." It was Soren's turn to grimace. "And back out into the field."

"Will it make me forget?"

"No. That would take more work. I wouldn't trust that sort of thing to anyone but the clinic on Targon. If you want that, I can put in a request for medical leave."

"No," Nova said at once. She touched her shoulder as if to test the darkening bruise. "I have no intention to forgetting any of this."

"Revenge, Lieutenant?"

"Not risking my career over that bastard. But that doesn't mean this is over, believe me."

"So you definitely want to report this?"

"Why wouldn't I?" Nova said angrily.

"Beryl runs this place. He keeps the grunts in line and functioning under some pretty extreme conditions. They don't want women in their ranks and they do whatever it takes to keep them out. You're a pilot and that's even more offensive to them. Frankly, I'm tired of patching up his victims and don't think they leave the new boys alone, either. If you're smaller or smarter, you're fair game. That's what it is here, Nova. You'll only make it worse for yourself by reporting it."

"I am not putting up with this!"

"Then get a transfer out of this pit. What are you doing out here, anyway?"

Nova dropped her forearm over her eyes. "Bellac wasn't exactly on my dream sheet. I want to get to Targon. I need the creds for that. And places like these are the fastest way to get them. I knew it's a pit. Just didn't think I'd have to watch out for our own people, too." She moved her arm again to peer at the doctor. "Did they get to you?"

"They tried. I made some noise about a few cases when I first got here. Some comments were made. I got the message." She sighed. "I'm not a soldier, I'm not an officer, and I'm not a pilot. I'm probably a coward. Once I have a few more points I'm out of here, too. Back to Siolet where they know how to run a military hospital. I stitch them up when they lacerate themselves and I don't get in their way. You're a target and they'll keep at you until you know your place." She fussed with her recorder and did not look at Nova. "I've seen it again and again. Sometimes I think this place is more like a prison than a military base. You get along or you get out, one way or another. Not everyone gets hurt, but it's the main routine. They don't have the smarts to find other ways to make your life intolerable." She tipped her head toward the door. "I had a chat with Lieutenant Tonda earlier. Somehow I don't think you're the sort that's easily intimidated. Admirable, but not likely to make your tour here all that much fun."

Nova grimaced. "Not exactly a vacation, so far, anyway."

* * *

"Whiteside! Step in here."

Nova nearly jumped off her metal bench when the base commander stepped into the hall to bark at her. He ignored her salute and returned to his cramped work room. When she followed she saw that she was alone in here with him. No other officer was there to take her deposition, no Doctor Soren, no peer witness to the proceedings. Just Major Trakkas, looking like he wished she'd never come onto his base.

"Sir," she said, standing stiffly beside the data console

where he had taken a seat. The rest of the room was lost in murk and clutter.

The Centauri officer scrolled through a few screens of information before turning to look at her. She ground her teeth when his violet eyes traveled slowly all the way down to her boots before moving up again. "I read the reports, Whiteside," he said.

"They were filed three weeks ago, sir," she pointed out. Three weeks of lewd remarks, speculating glances in her direction, whispered conversations, hostile looks and outright ostracism by some of her fellow soldiers. The only time she had felt at ease at all was among her wing, in the air, doing her job. The major finally summoned her only after, reluctantly, she had asked Captain Dakad to move the case forward. At least Beryl was on a mission to one of the Rim towns and she had not seen him since the night of the attack.

"I know what day it is, Lieutenant," he snapped. "This is a war zone. I have more burning issues than figuring out why you can't keep your door closed at night."

She gasped. "Sir?"

He waved his hand in a dismissing gesture. "What do you want, Whiteside?"

"What do you mean? Captain Beryl assaulted me. Raped me."

"He says you asked him into your room. That you like it rough."

Nova felt her anger rise and reminded herself to stay calm. The last thing that would help her now was to give in to her temper. "You know that isn't what happened," she said. "No matter what he told the rest of the base."

He observed her for an uncomfortably long time. "You think it's your job to stir things up here, Lieutenant? Wave protocol and policy under my nose when I have hundreds of Shri-Lan crawling like lice through civilian zones? We can't tell the damn difference between rebel and local because Targon won't let us expel off-worlders. My ground troops are being chewed up by weapons even you haven't seen,

Specialist," he added with a wave at her records, "and you want me to spend my time making sure everyone is playing nice here at the base?"

It's your damn job, she thought to herself and bit her tongue.

He let her wait while he continued to study her files. "Your psych assess looks all right," he said.

What did that mean? Because the base shrinks declared her fit this couldn't have been all that traumatic? She hadn't told them about the nightmares or about the gun she kept beside her bed now. They seemed happy with their tests and she got her plane back. After all, soldiers like Nova were trained for this, weren't they? Weeks of relentless, soul-numbing, body-breaking conditioning. Survival when captured, resistance under any condition, let nothing touch you, never give up. And, ladies, be prepared to be targeted for special treatment. Nothing said about being targeted by your own people.

Trakkas winced when something on the screen caught his attention. "Whiteside. I thought that sounded familiar when I first saw your name on the roster. Tegan Whiteside is your old man? *Colonel* Tegan Whiteside running the Pelion base?"

"Yessir."

He tapped his fingers thoughtfully on the console, his lips pursed. Finally, his eyes traveled back to her. "A colonel's daughter is what we have here. Now doesn't that make my day complete. No doubt a bit of noise from you is going to bring a whole lot of hurt down on our heads."

"Major, I—"

He held up a hand. "But you're not that sort, Whiteside. You're tough and you think you need to prove something. You'd rather put up with Beryl's entire squad than run crying to Daddy, isn't that so?" He leaned to the screen. "You did some ground combat against the Shri-Lan rebels on Phi, got your wings on Magra and then flew over Tannaday. Bucking for Hunter Class, I'm guessing. Weapons Specialist, just to show you have a big brain. There's no way your father would have dumped you onto this rock if he had any hand in your duty transfers. Because you won't let him, isn't that right? No special favors for Whiteside Junior. And you won't whine to him to get your ass out of here."

She said nothing. He was right.

He folded his hands behind his closely-cropped head and sat back in his chair, swiveling slowly side to side as he contemplated. "But unless he's a heartless bastard he probably has a pretty good idea what's going onto your record. Including your little misunderstanding with Captain Beryl."

She frowned. Up until this moment she hadn't even thought about her complaint against a superior officer showing up on her records. And although her father was hardly the warmest of Humans, he did not fall into the 'heartless bastard' category. He never interfered with her career choices but seeing this incident in her files would not go uninvestigated. 'Ironballs' Whiteside's reputation as a tough, uncompromising commander was widespread and no one would ever accuse him of ignoring policy. Her transfer into what he'd consider a safer tour of duty was guaranteed.

And she would agree. His wife, her mother, had been killed in a rebel attack on Magra only a few years ago and all that remained of his family in Trans-Targon was Nova. It was that reason, not any hope of favoritism, that kept her silent about some of her more hazardous assignments.

"Tell you what," Trakkas said. He looked like someone about to bestow a great favor upon lesser beings. "We'll downgrade this to a simple assault, I'll keep Beryl out of your way until your tour here is done, give him a slap to remind him of his manners, and we'll let this settle down naturally."

She glared at him. How did things get so turned around all of a sudden? "What sort of slap?"

He shrugged. "Twenty days in lockup."

"This is disgraceful! He damn near pulled my arm off!"

Trakkas came to his feet and towered over her, close enough to force her to take a step backward. "I am about done with you, Lieutenant. I'll give him thirty days. You know what that means? Thirty days without the toughest commander I have for these men. I'm going to have to pull Captain Tovah off the front line to take his place. Leaving me short in the field. So you, Lieutenant, are going to hump your ass out to Shon Gat and fill in the ranks."

She winced. The remote town he had named was the supply base for the nearby elevator construction. It was rapidly expanding in anticipation of the traffic and prosperity the tether would bring once the orbital skyranch was complete. It was also infiltrated by rebel factions deeply embedded among the local population and more arrived with each transport and caravan. Air Command presence had turned the entire place into a state of siege. Random attacks on military patrols, haphazard attempts at sabotage and days-long skirmishes were the order of the day. "I am a fighter pilot," she reminded him.

He laughed without any real semblance to humor. "You're also an expert marksman and I can definitely use more snipers. The Kites are done out here. There are no more rebel bases you can lob your little missiles at from a safe distance. And I have no intention of letting the pilots laze around until Targon decides what to do with you." His violet eyes gleamed with a mix of menace and mirth as he leaned over his workspace to enter his instructions. "You'll get a little education in how things really work on the ground, Lieutenant. Won't that be nice?"

"I've done ground combat," she said but there was little protest left in her voice. She had lost this battle.

"Good. You'll be useful. I think we both know it's probably best if you're not hanging around the base. Things won't get any friendlier for you once I lock Beryl up. Report to Captain Rudjo at the Shon Gat garrison tomorrow. Maybe he'll let you fly evac."

THREE

From up here, it was easy to see how this town might have been pretty once. Before the planet and her two moons had ever seen someone without white hair or red skin or carrying a laser weapon. Before interstellar travelers had discovered that rare fracture in space that let them form a jumpsite uncomfortably close to the planet. Before the rebels followed through the breach, smelling easy pickings and a shortcut from here to the hotly contested Magra-Aikhor sector.

Almost two hundred years, local time, after off-worlders had been accepted by the Bellac Tau natives, the population had grown into an uneasy mix of locals, Centauri, Feydans, and even some Humans. Cluttered composites of traditional brick architecture and imported construction made up the towns that sprawled along coasts and the fertile foothills, including this one, Shon Gat.

Nova sat on the running board of her hover, the screen of her scanner held loosely in her hands while she surveyed the town below. The original stone architecture still delineated the perimeter, as did parts of an ancient wall. Orderly pathways separated it into sectors organized according to who lived there or what they did. Neat residences, livestock areas, market places, meeting circles, open spaces were all still visible. Over time, the newcomers had blurred the boundaries. Modern trading places, machine shops, hover pads, military installations and not a few ragged slums had turned Shon Gat into the sort of sprawling, unmanaged frontier town she had seen in other places.

Of course, from up here, without moving in for a closer look, one did not see the areas destroyed by explosives or scorched by laser fire.

Since opening Bellac to off-world traffic so long ago, Air Command had found more important properties to protect elsewhere. The Union's advances toward bringing the remote planet into the Commonwealth had stalled again and again even as the rebel factions grew and multiplied. Now, both the Arawaj and Shri-Lan groups held firmly established territories here, well supplied by anti-Union sympathizers in other parts of the vast Trans-Targon sector.

Desperate to avoid becoming the official headquarters of Shri-Lan activities, the governors of Bellac Tau had appealed to the Union, offering control of the jumpsite in exchange. No one seemed to find it especially ironic that, if not for the Union itself, the planet would still be minding its herds and fisheries without even an inkling of worlds beyond its moons.

"Anything interesting?"

Her eyes returned to her scanner display when Tomos Reko came around the front of the airship. "Nothing. Caravan coming in from the north. No com noise from that. Rudjo sent a couple of skimmers out to meet them."

Entire tribes of nomads roaming the plains to trade their salt and animals meant a constant influx of new people into Shon Gat. Among them, protected by Air Command's mandate of non-interference with indigenous populations, traveled bandits and rebels. The best Union personnel could do was to inspect each caravan from a distance to make note of Bellacs with smoother skin, softer dialects, better equipment – all far more common in Ballac Tau's urban areas than out here.

The Centauri soldier leaned his rifle against the hover's

skids and slouched beside her. There was a fresh breeze up here in the rocky hills and both were glad to have left the dusty town for a while. Their endless patrols of Shon Gat's alleys in this heat covered their skin in a disagreeable paste of sweat and dust, all the more unpleasant for being trapped under their lightly armored combat suits. Both of them had removed their helmets although Nova still kept her bright red hair under a camouflage scarf.

"I say we stay up here a while longer, to make sure," he said, clearly enjoying his turn to partner with the only pilot in their platoon and spend the day in the sky. It was their job to display Air Command's physical presence in these hills, look for weapons caches, and investigate suspicious activity not easily detected through electronic surveillance.

"I think that's wise, Sarge." She scanned the flat horizon for signs of vehicles or power sources. All was quiet. She took her time with her visual inspection; some of the peculiar, pinkish salt pillars that rose from the ground like giant mushrooms could turn out to be a nomad on his desert beast. Or a rebel on a skimmer. "Nothing from the tether, either."

From here, the ground base of the elevator leading to the nearly completed skyranch, now settled into its synchronous orbit above the planet, was just a smudge in the distance. Her sensors showed vehicles and outbuildings and the massive perimeter fence, patrolled to ward off schemes by Shri-Lan rebels to hamper the construction. Nova's eyes followed the graceful line of the caged tether upward until it disappeared into the ever-present haze blanketing the planet.

Another condition for allowing the Union to control the nearby jumpsite was the construction of Skyranch Twelve and, soon, Thirteen. Solar power and light ensured a boundless crop of produce grown in microgravity to feed Bellac's growing and diverse population. The elevator guarded by their Air Command garrison delivered water, air, and supplies over a three day trip into space. Eventually, it would carry the orbiter's harvest and electricity surplus back down to the surface.

She looked up at the scanner on top of their hover while she adjusted it. Of course, providing a skyranch over Bellac also meant a very effective orbital communications and surveillance array for military use, making it a worthwhile expense.

"Too quiet, you think?" Reko reached back into the hover to fetch a bottle of water.

"Could be the heat." She accepted the bottle from him and pointed it at her screen. "Look. Caravan's stopping." They watched idly while the long line of people, animals, carts and a few well-used skimmers gathered into a tight knot. The smaller beasts where herded together in the center and most of the people got busy with digging a circle of shallow ditches. "Storm coming?"

Reko scanned the sky of the northern horizon. The nomads bred a peculiar sort of desert animal, short-legged crawlers called *churries* whose bodies were so flat and wide that they were actually used as shelters during a sandstorm. The herders merely dug a shallow depression into the sand and directed the ruminants to cover them. Efficient, warm, safe and probably not very sweet-smelling. Once the tan-colored animals settled on the ground, they became nearly impossible to spot from a distance.

"Want to bet that our skimmers aren't going to make it out there and back again before the storm hits?"

Nova smiled and tapped the com system on her data sleeve. "Base, Unit Four reporting herders digging in to the north-west."

"Heard, Four."

"You are spoiling my fun," Reko said but both of them knew that, if the caravan had been tipped off about the approaching patrol, the ditches might well be dug to hide rebel infiltrators. There had been no warning about an approaching sandstorm today and winds were calm over the plains. "Though if we get a storm we won't have to worry about an air strike today. They're not going to fly Shrills in here."

She nodded and sent a request for a more detailed weather analysis. Shrills, the small, single-seat fighters used primarily by the Shri-Lan, were nimble and powerful but far more delicate than Air Command's sturdy Kites. For days now, their scouts and spies had reported a possible air strike mobilizing on a continent outside Union influence. So far, the skies were empty of aircraft and would remain so during one of the choking sandstorms so common here.

But the rebels' most effective weapons were not machines of war. The methods that made Air Command's traditional operations useless in places like Shon Gat were rebel infiltrations into both civilian and military populations, explosives carried under clothing or lobbed with crude trebuchets, poisoned water, poisoned air, hostages and booby traps. Looking for threats inside the town and protecting the cadre of engineers working on the elevator base had become their main occupation.

Most overt rebel attacks featured elaborate schemes to disrupt the power transformers near the base. The tether itself was heavily shielded and bore missile defense mechanisms at intervals along its length, presenting a far more difficult target.

"Storm confirmed, Four," they heard from the direction of Nova's wrist. "Not until dusk, though. Proceed to Unit Five rendezvous point and overnight there."

"That storm's going to wreck my lungs for a week," Reko grumbled.

Nova reached over and tugged on his scarf. It was made of a flexible filtering material and she let it snap back against his face where it was most appropriately kept during a stand storm. "Maybe you should use the proper gear instead of trying to look suave without it," she said.

"I don't like to hide this pretty face."

"Your face, my boot." She ducked out of his way when he swung his arm to take her into a headlock. "You're far too slow, *shekka'an*."

He shook his head. "You need to put more emphasis on the last syllable," he instructed. "Really put feeling into that part to include my family. Much more insulting that way."

She practiced the Centauri expletive a few times until he was satisfied. "Now you got it. Stick with me, you'll go far."

She grimaced and looked out over the arid landscape. Scrubland from one horizon to the next, little grew here along the equator beyond what kept the local herd animals fed. Rocks, the occasional oasis of matted trees and mud-brick settlements, caravans. Far to the south in lusher landscapes, prosperous cities had sprung up with the wealth brought to Bellac by the Union. Out here little of that was in evidence. Of course, out here was one of the few places where the space tether could be built. The other was planned for a floating platform in the ocean, also along the equator.

He guessed her thoughts. "Can't wait to get out of here, huh?"

Nova shrugged. "I want to be in my plane." She gestured at the thin line the distant elevator etched into the sky. "We were told that we'd be patrolling the jumpsite and the new orbiter. Not blowing up Rhuwacs on the ground. Not beating up Bellac rebels that don't even know what they're fighting for. I'm less than sixty hours in the Kite away from qualifying for Hunter Class trials." She kicked at a stone to watch it tumble down the slope into the valley at approximately the same speed at which her hopes for quick advancement were disappearing. A Hunter Class pilot was practically guaranteed a post on some of the most desirable Air Command bases. Which, right now, was any place but Bellac Tau. "I've been waiting for that since I was about five."

"Just a few more days and you're back on the base," he reminded her. The members of Rudjo's company out here in Shon Gat had only a vague idea of why she had joined their squad. Not having been given a command, she had clearly not been promoted into this assignment. Rumors were mongered that she had gotten into an altercation with a senior officer but no one had asked for details. She was glad for that, also aware that a reputation for getting into brawls was probably helpful out here.

Then again, she had been relieved to find that the other grunts in her company were, for the most part, amicable and likable men who treated her as one of their own. Nova was not the only female combat soldier stationed here and her presence was not exceptional. This is what she had come to expect from her assignments, in the air or on the ground. There was no tolerance out here for those not doing their share to keep them all alive and so far she had given them no reason to doubt her abilities.

"Yeah, can't wait," she said. But was that even true? What was waiting for her back at the base? Captain Beryl whose personality probably hadn't improved after thirty days in lockup, his devoted followers who would surely find ways to retaliate, her own squad of pilots who'd probably rather not get into the middle of things. Despite what Major Trakkas had guessed about her, she was tempted to apply for transfer away from this dreary planet.

"You pilots have it made," Reko said. "Real beds, real showers, real food!"

"Sort of," she amended, her attention back on the screen in her hands.

"I'm thinking of quitting the military, did I tell you that?"

She nodded. He spoke of it daily.

"I'm heading back home to Magra. I have the sweetest girl in the world. She's a teacher. Languages, mostly. And music. Can you believe it? They teach music on Magra!" He smiled happily as he stared into the distance, perhaps in his mind seeing the planet from here. "I can get a job on the base, I think. Mechanics. What'll you do when you get out?"

She looked up, puzzled. Get out? Out of what? She had spent her entire life on one military installation or another, always assuming that that's what everyone did. Her father had moved his family to where he was posted, as was common among senior officers, and his only child had learned to adapt. Instead of music she had learned physics and ballistics and aviation. The languages she knew had come to her by listening to the rough talk of soldiers and cadets from a dozen different planets. Planes were her passion, weaponry her expertise. And not once had she thought about doing anything else. "Fly," she said.

"Boring, Whiteside! You need a hobby!" He put an arm around her shoulders and pulled her closer. His violet, mildly glowing eyes gleamed with mischief. "Hey, how about a boyfriend?"

Nova launched from her perch as if he had stuck a knife in her arm. "Don't!" she exclaimed before she caught herself.

He blinked, confused by her reaction. "Easy, Nova," he said, a hurt look on his face. "I'm just kidding around. I just told you I had a girl."

She took a deep breath and shook her head. "Sorry, just jumpy, I guess," she said although until this moment she had been perfectly at ease up here. "I know you didn't mean it."

Reko shrugged in an effort to make light of the awkward moment. "Of course I meant it. You're a pretty lady when you're cleaned up a bit, Lieutenant." He sighed dramatically and settled his helmet on his shaved skull. "Much too pretty for a Centauri grunt with a face like a boot."

Nova smiled. "Damn straight."

She packed up the remote scanner display and climbed after him into the hover plane. These compact vehicles were used to move silently among the hills, barely raising a plume of dust even at low altitudes. Not even remotely as powerful as her Kite, they were little more than a souped-up, armored skimmers, but at least she was airborne some of the time. It made her banishment to this isolated post more bearable than she had expected.

"Point the way, Sarge," she said when they had lifted off. He was studying their maps to look for the next destination along their surveillance route. After a moment he sent the information to the onboard navigator and she let the plane coast through a gap in the bluffs, away from Shon Gat and into the rugged hills to the south. Gradually, the foothills gave way to more densely-treed slopes. Ahead of them lay a saddle between some cliffs through which a narrow stream had carved its way through the ages. Beyond that, they knew, lay a village where they would rendezvous with another squad.

Nova tapped the ship's com system to hail them. "Do you think they've got any dinner for us?" she said to Reko. "I hear the people up there know how to roast those little goat-things without incinerating them."

"Probably helps to use a real fire. Would be nice to get some of that." Their quartermaster at the base had taken to purchasing herds of churries to augment the mess hall menu. Their use as an almost daily protein offering was decidedly underappreciated by the troops.

"Is everyone asleep up there?" Nova hailed the detachment again.

Reko looked up from his display. "No reply?"

"Nothing. From any of them." She tried an unencrypted com band. "Unit Five, come in. We're en route with your supplies. Got the ointment for your piles, Beamer, just so you're grateful."

Still no reply.

"I'm not liking this at all," she said. "Let's get a visual before we land."

They continued in silence. Nova scanned for airborne threats in the distance, Reko's attention was on the ground below them. They overflew gullies, rockfalls and several creeks meandering through the hills and onto the flats where the water sunk through fissures near Shon Gat to fill a vast subterranean reservoir.

"There," Reko said to his screens. "Those don't look like herdsmen. Groups of three or four, moving near the tree line."

"Are you sure?"

"Yeah. Weapons. And there's a troop moving two by two. Definitely not villagers." He zoomed the real vid for a closer look. "Rhuwac!" He cursed and reached for his rifle.

"Emphasis on the last syllable, remember?" She kept the plane low to keep them camouflaged against the backdrop of the hills. "We'll come back for them. I want to see what's going on up there before we start shooting Rhuwwies."

"I never get to have any fun," he grumbled but took his hands off the door he was about to slide open.

Nova signaled the base. "Unit Four here, Sarge. Rebel movement heading north toward Shon Gat. Counting Rhuwacs. No response from Unit Five. Taking a closer look."

"Negative," came the static reply after a moment. "Synchronized rebel attacks throughout Shon Gat. Casualties on both sides already. Everything south of the canal is blocked off. Return to base immediately. Join Reko's squad at the north gate when you get here."

"Heard, base."

"Look at this," Reko showed her his hand-held scanner. "Picking up two drum shields down there. What do they have that's so important?"

"Crap!" Nova swung the hover around hard enough to make Reko grab for the console to steady himself. "Coilers."

"Out here?"

She did not reply, busy with swooping in an erratic pattern away from the bluffs. But this wasn't a Kite and they were close enough to touch, it seemed. Reko had no further objections when they saw the tracer with its telltale spiral pattern angle toward them. It whipped by close enough to rock the plane in its wake. She climbed higher and pushed the hover to its limits to escape the next volley from the ground. "We're one great big target up here."

Reko said nothing, unaccustomed to trusting his life to a vehicle never meant for engagement. No shielding, limited armaments, an explosive fuel tank at his back – it suddenly seemed safer on the ground, taking one's chances with the Rhuwacs.

She had finally come about and headed back to Shon Gat,

taking the most direct path through the valley. The plane's system reported incoming laser fire from the rebel groups that Reko had spotted on the way up.

"Feel free to pop yourself some Rhuwacs, Reko," she yelled.

"Are you crazy! I'm not opening that door with you flying like this. Just get us out of here!"

She punched his arm. "Use the onboard guns. It'll at least distract them."

Reko returned the fire as well as he could through her twitching evasive maneuvers while she hailed their commander. "Base, this is Unit Four. We took fire below Sarasun. Sighted two anti-aircraft positions. Clear now and approaching from the south."

"Heard," came the static reply after a moment. "That's a no-fly over Shon Gat for now. Land at the lift."

Nova and Reko listened to a burst of static and cross-traffic that included the sound of some very large explosions. "*Cazun*," he whispered. "What's going on down there? Did they get tired of trying to get at the transformers?"

"Must have been filtering people in for weeks now," she said. They now saw the town ahead of them, forming a broad triangle as it spread out from the base of the hills into the plains. Dust or smoke billowed into the air from more than one location. "You'd think those damn caravans—"

"Incoming!"

A shudder went through the hover and then alarms started to complain from the console in front of them. Whatever had hit them sent it into a wobble which she corrected quickly but the indicators showed a steady and troublesome power loss. "Not going to make it," she yelled.

"What the hell does that mean!"

"We have to land, what do you think it means? Hang on to something."

He groped for the seat restraints while she fought with the hover's definite preference for landing at a problematic velocity. She worked quickly to override some of the automated scripts which, although faithful to safety protocols, were useless now. The hover started to shimmy dangerously as she dropped lower. It tilted, corrected, and then landed with a thump.

They sat still for a moment, stunned by the realization that they were still alive.

"Damn, you're adequate, Whiteside," Reko said finally with a forceful exhalation of air.

Something whistled overhead and then an explosion sent a shower of rocks and dust over the hover.

"Out," Reko said. "They'll want the hover and they can have it. But not with us in it."

They grabbed their guns and gear to abandon the vehicle. There should have been Air Command patrols all along this end of town but they saw no one. In the distance the decommissioned shuttle they had been using for their patrols stood open and deserted, its com array a twisted wreck. Someone lay sprawled halfway down its entrance ramp.

"Which way," she said. With a half dozen years of combat behind him, Reko's instincts on the ground were something to study and emulate and she was bothered not one bit about outranking the sergeant on this mission.

"Into town," he replied after studying the terrain for a moment. "We won't be as easily found as out here. Might have to ditch the uniforms."

A rattle of gunfire tore up the ground not far to their right, leaving them little choice but to go with Reko's suggestion. They ran toward the first of the low buildings, dodging fences and farm animals along the way. Once past the first of the structures, they entered a maze of alleys that had never had to accommodate anything wider than a push cart. The single-storied houses huddled close to each other, made of some mortarless arrangement of interlocking triangular bricks common to this part of Bellac Tau.

An explosion shook the ground under their feet.

"Let's get indoors and figure out where we are." Reko rapped a fist on the wooden door of one of the buildings.

No one answered.

Nova checked the scanner on her data sleeve. "Three in there. Bellacs. Hiding in a back room." She looked around the empty alley, deserted by locals who cowered in their darkened homes, hoping to be bypassed by both rebels and soldiers alike. Distantly, explosions thundered at uneven intervals and the sharper rapport of projectile weapons added to the sounds of battle. "Everything past that is jammed. We won't get through to the base in here."

He tried another door, with the same result. "While we were expecting an aerial attack from the desert, they're sneaking in the back door through the hills. And what's with those guns? Damn coilers? Who's selling those to Shri-Lan these days?"

"And who's adapting them. They're not even designed to work in this gravity. Seen them take down a Kite a while back. Just drilled through the skin." She raised her arm to attempt a com link to the base when they heard voices. Someone slammed a door nearby. They ducked when something whistled overhead. A dud, apparently – no explosion followed. The quick slap of sandaled feet came from the alley, followed by the sound of guns. Someone screamed.

Rifles in hand, Nova and Reko moved silently into the next alley where they found a thickly-robed Bellac male sprawled on the ground, moving his limbs in a feeble attempt to crawl toward a nearby doorway. She knelt beside him while Reko stood guard.

She hissed when the man on the ground raised a pistol to her throat. Instinctively, she moved to disarm him when a blinking blue light above his finger caught her attention.

"Flash!" she gasped and recoiled. Reko, too, stepped back when the man, little more than a youth, scrambled to his feet.

He gripped the pistol in both hands, arms stretched out toward them. Three other boys appeared by his side, also wielding guns. They were dressed in the loose robes of the desert nomads but the yellow dye in their hair was more common in the towns. "We are Shri-Lan!" he shouted in his native Bellac dialect. "You are hostages. Guns. Down!"

Nova spread her hands out from her body and dropped her rifle. "Look," she said as calmly as she could manage, aware that her command of Bellac mainvoice was barely passable. "That gun might not be what you think it is."

"Shut up!" he waved his pistol at Reko. "Down the gun. Down the gun."

The sergeant complied. Nova tapped the side of her helmet to drop the sun shield over her eyes. "Shri-Lan," she tried again, using the term to flatter him although she found it unlikely that the rebels would use these urchins for anything more than messengers or servants. "See that blue light on the side of your gun? It means that the setting on that pistol is set to wide flash. It uses light waves—"

"I know what it does!" he yelled. His hands shook as he tried to look at the indicator. His companions, carrying more conventional rifles, also glanced nervously in his direction.

"I just want to make sure," she said. "Because when that goes off, we all die. You need a special sort of eye shield to use it."

"Liar. Get up against that wall! Back off!"

Nova nodded to Reko and they stepped back further, away from their dropped weapons. "Just switch it off, to another setting," Nova tried again. "There is a slider under the tab by your thumb—"

A shot rang out, impossibly loud in this narrow alley and then Reko was on his knees, clutching his side. The youth who had fired pointed his gun at Nova. "You think we are scared of Air Command?"

"Why did you do that, Moks?" another boy exclaimed. Reko dropped to the dusty floor, groaning in pain as he covered the wound with his hands.

Nova raised her hands, worried by the thugs' panicked expression, especially on the face of the one with the flash module. "Just tell us what you want," she said. "No need to hurt anyone."

"We are Shri-Lan," the shooter said with little conviction, his eyes on Reko and the growing puddle of blood in the dust.

"Shut up!" his comrade snapped. He stepped closer to Nova. "Your scanners, your side arms, the com bands. Take it all off. Now." He pointed at her thigh. "And that knife. Quick."

She removed her hardware and handed the tools to the one named Moks. He chortled gleefully and disappeared between two buildings with his treasures. The other stripped Reko of his equipment and followed, leaving her alone with just two of the boys.

"You have our things," Nova said. "Now let me take care of my partner."

"You are coming with us to Arter, Union scum," he shouted.

Nova nodded in resignation and turned to step around Reko, making a small stumbling move as if to avoid stepping on him. In that instant she snapped her hand toward the flash gun wielder to grasp his wrist and push him back up against a brick building. She shoved her body against his, pinning the lethal weapon between them. Dangerous only when visible, the gun's deadly radiation would be smothered by his robe. She used her free forearm to press his face against the wall.

"Shoot her!" the youth grunted at his remaining compatriot. That one stared open-mouthed at their strangely intimate contact, glanced at Reko writhing on the ground, turned and fled.

Nova felt, more than heard, one of the boy's fingers crack as she bent it away from the gun. Yelping in pain, he gave up his grip and she pulled away with it. She silenced him with a few quick punches and then disabled the gun. The only sound in the alley now was the distant rumble of guns and her hoarse gasps for air.

"Reko!" She knelt beside the sergeant. "Talk to me!"

He groaned. "No big damage, I think. I hope. *Cazun*, this

hurts! Where the hell did those kids get a flash mod! That's just crazy."

She peered at his injury and managed to let none of her apprehension show on her face. "Come on, we have to keep moving. Let's find a place to lay low for a while. This riot can't last forever."

She spun when she felt the unmistakable contact of a gun jabbing into her ribs. Someone's boot shoved her backward and she tumbled over Reko into the dirt. He cried out in pain. When she tried to scramble to her feet the tracers of two guns honed in on her chest and face.

Six armed men and women, four of them Centauri and two Bellac, surrounded them now. One of them held Nova's own rifle and the boy that had disarmed her just a few minutes ago hovered behind them. He spotted his friend sprawled in the dust across the alley. "She's killed Joah!"

"He's not dead," Nova said without taking her eyes off the newcomers. These were not locals, judging by the mix of weapons and clothing originating on a half dozen different planets. The two Bellacs had dyed their hair to a dull ash, no doubt to blend into the dun desert landscape.

One of the Centauri gestured with his gun. "We'll take both of them. Might be worth something to Air Command."

"I'd say she is, anyway," another said and let her tracer drift toward Nova's insignia. "Pilot."

"Out here? Probably won those wings in a game." The Centauri stepped over Reko and relieved Nova not only of the flash gun but also her insignia and tags. "Move that way. Keep your hands where we can see them."

FOUR

Nova watched them lift Reko from the ground, unmindful of his injuries and deaf to his moans of pain. Guns remained trained on her when she was marched from the alley. The rebels moved without bothering to duck for cover even as missiles shrieked overhead. As far as Nova was able to tell, the shells were lobbed from inside Shon Gat toward the garrison to the north. But she was hustled along so quickly and through so many twists and bends between buildings that all looked alike that she was soon lost. Their captors eventually turned into an arched doorway leading into a flat-roofed building extending for an entire block down the street.

Nova stopped abruptly when she saw the mayhem before of them. The interior seemed to consist mostly of one large hall, little more than a bunker or perhaps a warehouse, unadorned and with few furnishings. Narrow windows allowed a few dusty beams of daylight in here and a string of lights brightened the far corners. Everywhere she looked, crude pallets were lined up on the floor and on those lay dozens of people, all of them in obvious distress. The smell of disinfectant, gore and vomit hung heavily in the air. From everywhere in this hall the sound of people in pain and fear mingled into a nightmarish drone.

She was shoved aside when several people, all of them Bellac, rushed in with a stretcher made of some sort of carpet slung between long poles. The woman carried on it muttered something in a thick dialect that was beyond Nova's training but her pain and fear was clearly written on her face. Her leg was covered in blood-soaked bandages.

"You there. Human." The Centauri leader of her captors waved to a man dressed in a stained medical smock. "You're responsible for her."

"What the hell does that mean?" Nova said angrily. The medic was unarmed and, although solidly built, not especially threatening.

"Means that if you don't do what you're told, he'll have less work to do around here." The rebel grasped her arm and dragged her to where another casualty lay unconscious on a rug. He bent and put his gun to the man's head. "Let me show you."

"Stop that!" Nova cried, aghast.

"Please!" The medic he had pointed out rushed over to them. "This isn't necessary." He inserted himself between the rebel and his victim. "She gets it. No need for a demonstration."

The rebel rose and held the muzzle of his pistol to Nova's neck. "Make sure she does. Her soldier pal is expendable, too. Clear now?"

She jerked her head away from his gun. "Clear."

He smirked and turned to the Human. "She's probably had some training so put her to work till we need her." The rebel left abruptly and without further instructions.

Nova glared after him.

"Just do as he says." The man who had not been introduced to her shrugged. "We can use the help, anyway. This all happened so fast, whatever it is that's happening out there." He lifted his hands to encompass the injured people in the hall.

Nova followed his gesture, but not to study the casualties. Instead, she counted the number of armed rebels at the exits and the distance to the open windows. "Where is the other officer they brought in?"

"He's being looked after." He caught the arm of a young woman passing by with an armload of rags. "Go with Coria. Get rid of that uniform and wear whatever she gives you. Let's not remind everyone of who you are."

The woman named Coria took a moment to scrutinize Nova, her disapproval evident. Finally, she gestured for her to follow and led the way along a dark hallway into another room, a supply area. She dug through a tangle of clothing on the floor while Nova went to the only window and peered outside.

"Don't try it," the Bellac said, like her colleague fluent in the mainvoice used universally by the Commonwealth. "They've got Rhuwacs out there."

"Are you Shri-Lan?" Nova said.

"I'm a weaver."

"But you're working for them. Helping them."

The woman handed her a bundle that turned out to be a loosely fitting pair of trousers gathered at the ankles. "You didn't notice the guns, Officer? I'd rather be at my looms. Your Union has other plans for us."

"Our Union? We did not attack you."

"No. You attack each other. And we just happen to be in the way. Without you, there'd be no rebels here. Without you, there'd be no rebels anywhere. Most of the people dying out there on the floor are not rebels, either. They are my neighbors. My friends. We grab up who we can and bring them here. And if there are rebels among them, so be it. Air Command is quick to collect their own. You won't find many of your people here."

Nova frowned. "Surely, we don't leave the locals lying in the street."

Coria stood with her hands on her hips and peered at Nova through narrowed eyes. Like all Bellacs, her skin was a deep, burnished red, making her white dye-free hair all the more startling in contrast. The long braids gathered up high on the back of her head stood stiffly to point in all directions. "Just the rebels? How do you tell the difference?"

Nova shrugged. There was no answer to the woman's question. It was all too easy for rebels of any species to work their way into Union populations. She unfastened her fatigues and exchanged them for the pants and a flowing overvest that reached to her knees. "What happened? What started this today?"

"Stupidity, what else? Rebels been creeping into town for weeks. Recruiting new members, mainly. Sifting into the population. Getting supplies and disappearing into the hills again. Then there was talk about one of the big Shri-Lan bosses organizing things right here in Shon Gat."

"They wouldn't dare so close to the base," Nova said, incredulous.

"Of course not. But that rumor, if you want to call it that, gave your people excuse to march in here and start going door to do looking for rebels." The woman took Nova's uniform and stuffed it into a bag before handing it back to her. "So the Shri-Lan fought back and things got ugly fast. And the people of this town suffer for it. Again."

The Bellac gestured for Nova to return with her to the main hall. She stopped again at the end of the dim corridor. "Don't forget for a moment that you are their prisoner here. A hostage. If they didn't want you for something you'd be dead by now. I advise you not to play Union Soldier around here. If you escape they will kill some of us, any of us, to set an example. I don't suggest you try."

Nova nodded absently as she scanned the crowded space, searching for Reko among the injured. There had to be a way to contact her unit. And surely some of these people would know a relatively safe way to get through the front lines. Some of the injuries she saw required far more extensive attention than what seemed available in this crude clinic.

"They would have taken your friend around that bend,"

Coria pointed.

Nova picked her way through the pallets on the floor to a less crowded section near the back. It was out of sight from the main entrance and darker. She finally spotted Reko, barely conscious on a thin mattress that was too short for his gangly Centauri frame. Someone had stripped him of his uniform jacket and covered him with a dusty blanket.

"Tomos," she whispered, crouching beside him. "You in there?"

He blinked up at her and tried a lopsided grin. "Yeah. What is this place? Evac?"

"No. Med station. Patrolled by rebels to make sure their people get treated first. Looks like mostly Bellacs working here." She tried not to wince when she lifted the thick pad of dressing from his side. "You're missing a chunk of meat there," she said. "I'll try to find a scanner to get a better look."

"You do that, Lieut—" he frowned, reminding himself that they were among rebels. "Nova."

She looked up when someone knelt beside her. It was the Human who was apparently responsible for her upon pain of death. He began to replace Reko's bandages, expert in his task in spite of large, blunt-fingered hands. "We have one scanner here and it's not a good one. But the doctor said this is just a bad bleeder. We need to get that stitched up."

"Stitched?" Nova said. "That'll need a graft. You have no equipment here at all?"

"Not a lot. Your friend here didn't rate highly in triage." Nova realized that he was younger than he first appeared. Unlike herself, whose skin was exposed to the sun only on the occasional ground mission, he was deeply tanned and his light hair seemed bleached by weather. His body was dense and powerful, like that of someone used to working outdoors. He smiled wistfully. "I suppose that's a good sign."

"They gave me a shot of the good stuff," Reko said. "Not feeling much pain now." He nudged her arm. "You have to get out of here, Nova. Get back to the base and get help."

"I'm not leaving you, Sergeant. Bet on that."

The medic gave a snort of derision. "There is no way in or out of here without sacrificing more civilians, anyway. You know that and they know that. You'll have to be our guests for the next little while."

"This has got to blow over soon," Nova said.

"Not until your people get some backup, I'm guessing." He shrugged. "I guess your elevator is more important than a few townsfolk."

"They attacked the tether base?"

He seemed amused. "I'm probably much less interested in warfare strategies than you are. We are a little too busy for that sort of thing around here." The tilt of his head pointed out the disorder around them. "And could use a hand until someone gets this under control."

"All right." She gave Reko's hand an assuring squeeze and rose. "You get some sleep, if you can. We'll get out of here soon enough. Don't worry."

Reko squinted up at the medic. "They teach them to say that crap in officer school, you know."

"I thought it sounded a little rehearsed."

She followed the man down an aisle between the rows of cots and into a makeshift dispensary. The shelves were nearly empty. "He called you Nova?" he said, handing her a plastic smock and a supply of gloves. "That's quite a name to live up to."

She watched him count out single-dose ampules of medication. "I had a bit of a temper as a child. What's your name?"

"Nathon Lis Djari, formerly of the Tangmak Rift but currently stuck here in Shon Gat, as you can see. You can call me Djari." He smiled, something that seemed to come easily to him, even here. "And I will call you Sunshine. Far less explosive a name, I think."

"You're a poet," Nova mumbled as she pulled the smock over her head. "And a doctor?"

"I can only wish, on both counts. I'm a farmer.

Apparently I took a wrong turn when the shooting started. I hope that Centauri was right when he said you might have some training?"

"Just basic medical. I don't know much about Bellacs at all. And you have a lot of them here."

"I guess we'll learn together. Just follow the doctors around. They'll tell you what they need."

They returned to the main ward. She scanned the hall to take a closer look at the few armed rebels loitering near the exit. All of them were Bellac natives, indistinguishable from the neutral population except for their guns. By their stance and demeanor, none of them were trained for this. And none of them seemed inclined to help with the wounded.

An excited babble of voices reached them, speared by a high-pitched wail that sounded the same at the edge of every battlefield. The rebel guards stood aside to allow another stretcher to enter, carried by several harried civilians. A distraught older woman seemed to want to help and impede their progress all at once.

"Come," Djari said and rushed toward them. He waved at the men to carry the stretcher to an open spot on the floor where a stained mattress had only recently been vacated. Nova helped to transfer the injured youth, wincing over the lack of clean supplies for these people.

The boy, his hair a wild pattern of blue and violet streaks, howled in pain and weakly fought to keep them from checking his wounds. "Hold him down," Nova snapped to one of the men. She tore the blood-soaked shirt to reveal a bullet wound. The woman behind her cried out at the sight. Nova grabbed a handful of bandages from someone and pressed them into the wound. She looked over to Djari kneeling beside her and saw that he understood the hopelessness of this injury. "That's not an Air Command weapon," she said quietly. They raised the boy's shoulder and she felt beneath him. "Shot in the back."

"We can't help him," Djari said. He glanced up at the woman. "I'll try to find something for the pain until…" he trailed off and stood up. For a moment he just gazed over the rows of pallets. Perhaps he meant to say something more but then he turned and walked away.

Nova covered the boy's injuries and then motioned to the woman who had come in here with him. The others had gone, leaving only the quietly weeping Bellac at his side when Nova turned her attention to another casualty.

And so it went. Victim after victim needed medicines they did not have, water they had to ration, equipment that just did not exist in this part of town. Nova did what she could, using her rudimentary training to patch up laser burns, bullet wounds, lacerations and broken bones. There were just two doctors here and a handful of medics. Even the basic scanner in her lost data sleeve was more adept than the single diagnostic tool they had here. She worked at Djari's side to move victims, clean equipment and tools, carry out the doctors' orders and distribute what little food was brought in by the locals.

"Sunshine," Djari whispered when, hours later, she walked past him to fetch more saline from their meager stores. He gestured urgently.

She squatted beside him to peer at an unconscious Bellac that had just been brought in. Her hair was dyed a muted tan color and she wore a patched set of fatigues. Nova whistled soundlessly when Djari parted the rebel's jacket to expose a belt studded with concussion charges. Unfortunately, the weapon they belonged to was not also with her. They worked quietly as if seeing to some injury while slipping the blunt cylinders into Nova's trouser leg. She flinched when she felt Djari's fingers brush over the bare skin of her calf but he had been working with the ill and injured for so long that he probably didn't even notice.

She rose, hoping the charges wouldn't rattle as she walked. Djari caught her hand. "Bring back a splint for her arm."

She looked down at the Bellac, frowning.

Djari squeezed her hand. "She's not a rebel right now,"

he said. His soft gray eyes shifted to their patient. "She's someone who's going to be in a whole lot of pain when she wakes up. Let's not add to that."

"Are all farmers as big-hearted as you are?"

His brows drew together and he released her hand. "Sometimes I think it's only us farmers that care about any living thing these days. Would I do anything less for her than I would for some livestock?" He patted a damp cloth on the woman's face where a massive bruise was forming. "Would anyone risk this if they didn't have some reason, some cause, whether I understand it or not?"

Nova nodded. "I'll hurry." She made her way to the corner where Reko was resting uncomfortably on his pallet.

He tried to sit up when she lowered herself beside him but soon gave up. "Nice of you to visit."

"How are you doing?" she said, tugging on the cuff of her trousers.

"Like there's someone chewing on my ribs. Doc doesn't think they can stitch that up. Going to be one hell of a scar."

"Maybe it'll be a dashing one. You can brag about it."

"What have you got there?"

She briefly held up one of the charges. "Are you up to a bit of tinkering?"

"I think so. Not exactly my field, though."

She tucked all but one of the cylinders under his blanket. "Easy. Open this end; I'll try to find you something to pry it with. There will be two wires in there, leading to this ring. Pull out the one that looks coppery. Might be hard to see in this light, so be careful. It'll make the thing explode on impact without the gun. Convert only half of these, just in case we do get our hands on a pistol for it."

He looked doubtful. "Can those explode on me?"

"No, you have to bash them hard enough to break."

"So you say. Are there a lot of rebels here?"

"Hard to say. Some are easier to spot than others. They're not talking much if they are."

"Try to get some intel, anyway. I feel totally useless lying around here, not knowing what's going on out there. Did I hear Rhuwacs earlier?"

"Yeah, there are a few of them outside, making sure we don't leave. There are two other Union soldiers here, both badly burned and going nowhere. At this point I'm guessing we're all hostages. I'm not hearing a lot of artillery now."

He nodded. "Maybe they're talking. I sure would like to see the inside of a real hospital right about now."

She rose to return to work. "You and a few dozen others. I'll bring you some water."

The hall had grown dark and stifling once the promised sand storm reached the town and the windows were shut tightly against it. Thankfully, the weather also seemed to have halted the battle and the arrival of new casualties slowed to a trickle. Nova helped to deliver a baby amidst the chaos; a new experience that left her both shaken and amazed. Hours passed and they seemed like days. Blood, tears, filth. Nova moved numbly through her chores, resolved to let her body do the work and keep her mind from taking in what she saw here. She felt unequipped to comfort those who came in more shell-shocked than injured and left those to the more gentle ministrations of Djari and his people.

His capacity for caring for these broken and frightened people seemed infinite. Nova found herself watching and, she realized, learning more from him than the doctors. His smile was sincere and applied at just the right time, his touch soothing and cool, his voice calm. His patience remained when Nova herself wanted to shout at a hysterical husband or snap at a helper for making errors. But he was as fatigued as anyone else here and she saw an expression of despair and even anger creep over his face more and more frequently.

Not wanting to act the officer among these people, Nova finally enlisted Coria's help to organize the exhausted workforce into shifts so that some of them could get some rest.

Dawn was not far off when she returned to Reko's corner to check his wound.

"What's going on, Nova," he mumbled when she replaced his bandages.

"Still the same. Did you get those charges done?"

"Yeah. Under my knee. Get anything useful?"

"Not much. Air Command is sniping at the front line to keep them busy but the bombing has stopped. Rebels keep shoving civilians and Rhuwacs at them. We've seen this before." She looked at her hands that burned and had turned rough with the use of the harsh disinfectants. She had seen battle and she had been part of it. What she had not seen were places like these, hidden away behind the front line where people came to die, to have shattered limbs removed, to await arrest by Air Command who rarely backed out of a battle once begun. To know that they existed was a long way from living in one.

He accepted a cup of water. "Command's not going to risk pissing off the governors by taking the town back by force." He squinted up at her. "No offense, Lieutenant, but you look terrible."

"Thanks." She pulled up a blanket she had found somewhere and curled up beside him. "I could sleep for a week. What do you think Command will do with this place?"

"Wait them out, maybe. Cut off food supplies. By now they're probably evacuating as many of the locals as possible. Could end up dropping a little dust if the weather clears."

Nova groaned. The 'dust' he referred to would, when dropped from overhead, blanket the town in a relatively fast-acting aerosol drug that would temporarily incapacitate rebel and civilian alike. Its effectiveness depended on how intent their enemy was on taking revenge on the locals before succumbing to it. She had been deployed for that tactic just last year, over Tannaday. It had left her feeling intensely unclean.

"It'd be a last resort," he said. "They won't like the idea of more coilers in here somewhere and the storm isn't going to let up for a while. We're definitely looking at no-fly. Did you get anything useful from the rebels?"

"Not much. Sounds like they've pretty much used up the Rhuwacs they brought. The tether hasn't been compromised but that's no surprise. Someone said that one of the transformers got blown, though."

"Any objective?"

"Same crap. They're trying to get Bellac's governors to give up on the Union. Refuse the alliance and keep the jumpsite neutral. Without a Union relay station at the gate. As usual, they've got nothing to bargain with." Nova closed her eyes but an image of a little girl that had come in earlier kept appearing behind her lids. There had been blood in the stiff little braids on the child's head. "I have no idea why this blew up today, though."

"Yes, seems odd. Unless someone really fouled up, I don't see the win here."

* * *

Nova awoke a few hours later to the sound of roars and curses outside. There were no windows at this end of the building but she made out Rhuwacs and the voices of their handlers. She pulled her blanket over her head for a moment to block the ugly noise, hoping what she was hearing didn't mean the end of a captive's bid for escape.

She sat up, eventually, blinking and rubbing eyes that stung from exhaustion and the dust still hanging in the air from last night's storm. The light of dawn had found its way into the hall and some of the others moved among the injured, waiting for their turn to sleep a little. She rose and bent over Sergeant Reko. But he had not awoken to the noise and when she touched his face it was hot and dry. She cursed quietly and checked his injury.

"Morning, Sunshine. How is he doing?"

Nova looked up when Djari joined her. He didn't look like he had slept much these past few hours, either, but his striking smile seemed to brighten this corner. "Got infected," she said and bit back another profanity. For some reason it seemed to her that this man probably didn't care much for foul language even among soldiers.

He checked Reko's temperature by touch. "Maybe today we'll get out," he said. "It's been quiet." He shrugged when another Rhuwac bellow seemed to shake the walls. "Except for them, anyway."

"Your optimism is spooky, you know that?" Nova dipped a cloth into a basin of almost clean water to cool Reko's face.

He watched her use the rag to wipe the back of her own neck. "What else is there?" he said quietly and she wished she hadn't spoken. "How else can you live like this? How can anybody?"

"Nobody is *supposed* to." She hesitated before placing her hand on his arm. "You're right, we'll get out. These things run their course."

He gazed at her without speaking and somehow that made her blush. Glad for the inadequate light, she dropped her eyes and pulled her hand back to fuss with Reko's bandages. "So what's a Human civilian doing all the way out here in Shon Gat? You seem a little out of place here."

"I am," Djari agreed. "I was born on the base at Siolet. My father was killed when I was still very young. My mother eventually took up with a Bellac farmer and moved out to the Tangmak Rift. *Anai* root and some livestock."

"You're a long way from Tangmak."

"Know why I'm here?" He looked as if about to reveal a great secret. "Trying to get to the skyranch. I've asked for work up there. Already talked to some administrators. I know what Bellacs like and I know how to grow it. I've been studying up on moisture recyclers, hydroponics, soilless farming. I'm practically hired already!"

"You'll like it up there, I'm sure," she said, touched by his excitement. "I've lived on a skyranch or two. They try to make them interesting enough for the workers and engineers. It's like a little town up there. And with the jumpsite so close you'll meet some interesting people."

The sound of harsh voices startled both of them. She peered into the gloom to see several Centauri and a few

Bellac, all seemingly in good shape and not part of the medical team, walk among the injured. One of them was barking orders at the others.

"What could they want now?"

"That tall fellow is Phann Arter, one of their leaders. He came in from Camomas with his group a few days ago. Looks like they're removing the rebels that can walk on their own. Maybe they're leaving. Or maybe they've run out of fighters."

"Air Command isn't likely to let them leave. By now the town will be surrounded." She scowled. "Nobody here is in any shape to fight."

"Maybe not by your standards. But his people are fanatics."

She stood up. "I can be pretty fanatical, too."

"Where are you going?" he called after her when she strode into the main section of the hall and toward the bellowing Centauri. She did not reply; thinking about this would only change her mind.

"Are you in charge here?" she said to the heavily armed rogue. He was of a heftier build than was common among his towering but generally slender people, adding a frightening dimension to his surly demeanor. It took a moment for him to realize that she was addressing him.

"What?" he said, somehow making that word sound like a growl.

"I want to speak to someone who is able to do a bit more around here than point his gun at things," she said. Djari had come around to the side and watched with an expression of sheer terror when the leader turned to face her.

"What do you have to speak about, Human?" the rebel said.

A Caspian strolled over to watch the exchange. He carried a medical scanner, apparently looking for those well enough to be removed from the clinic.

"What did Siks have to say?" the Centauri giant asked him.

"Progress," the Caspian said, using his native language. "The place is deserted. Some flyovers but we're not seeing any patrols on the ground. Looks like everyone is here now. Sloban's going to hit it tonight."

Nova managed to keep her reaction to this information to herself. A diversion? All of this? She squared her shoulders. "These people are suffering. Two more died last night. Look at this! We don't have enough supplies to help them all. Some of them are your people." She gestured at the thinly-furred rebel beside him. "None of the medics know how to treat Caspians. We're running out of clean bandages and disinfectant. There isn't enough food. The water is probably tainted. We need scanners and decon wands. We can only type Bellac and Centauri blood and there isn't enough of that, either. By the end of the day we won't even have enough pain meds to let them die in peace. This has to stop."

Arter's forehead lowered into deep grooves as he contemplated the angry woman before him. He turned to his companion. "I think that's her. Has to be Air Command, with a lip like that on her."

The Caspian nodded. His yellow eyes narrowed; perhaps he was worried about the information he had just slipped to his leader. "What's your name, Human?" he asked, using his own language as before.

"Speak so I can understand you," she said. "Centauri or mainvoice will do."

Before she could react, he grasped her wrist to turn her forearm outward. She winced when he stabbed her with a small tool and then released her again.

"What was that for?" she said, rubbing her arm.

"Not a lot of Humans in these parts," Arter said. "Your people are looking for an MIA soldier. Little pilot girl. Sound familiar?"

"Don't know what you're talking about," she said. She watched the Caspian enter the sample he had taken from her into his scanner. She glared at Arter. "That's the kind of equipment I'm talking about."

They ignored her until the Caspian tapped the display. "Yes, that's her." He reached out and tugged the scarf from her head to reveal her tousled red hair before activating a small device on his chest to make a video recording of her. His leader stepped outside camera range. "Done," the Caspian said after working with his equipment. "Sent."

"You're lucky Air Command wants you back, girl," Arter said. "Seems they don't want to talk to the likes of us until they know you're alive. Where's the other one?"

"Dead by this evening if you don't listen to me and find us more to work with," Nova said. "At least get us a scrubber so we can have clean water. Let us take the children out. Air Command will take care of them."

The two rebels turned away.

"Dammit, I'm talking to you, Centauri!" she snapped.

The hulking rebel leader turned back, moving very slowly. His huge fist reached out to wrap around her neck. He tightened it. "We are a little busy, Human. And I'm not in the mood to be shouted at by a Union soldier. Do you get that or do I have to snap your scrawny neck?"

She did not take her eyes from his, nor did she struggle to get out of his iron grip. After a thoughtful silence, he let her go with a small shove.

When he turned away again he waved at some of his men. "Get them a scrubber and get whoever is left in this dump to find some food." Impatiently, he snatched the scanner from the Caspian's hands and thrust it at Nova before stomping to the exit. "None of the civilians are to leave. Get this place cleaned up!"

Nova slumped against the wall, coughing and clutching her prize to her chest. Her knees suddenly seemed awfully wobbly.

Djari came to wrap an arm around her waist to hold her up. "That is either the stupidest thing I've ever seen or the bravest. Or maybe a bit of both." He pulled the computer from her hands and gave it to one of the medics who immediately hurried away with it.

"Stupidest."

They looked up when Coria, his Bellac colleague, approached. "The last time someone annoyed them they took five of us outside. They're still out there, unburied." She scowled at Nova. "I told you not to play Air Command soldier around here. You'll get us all killed."

Nova pulled out of Djari's loose embrace. "What I got you is a scanner and clean water. If things don't improve soon we'll have dysentery to deal with as well." She turned to Djari. "Centauri have a weak spot. You can tell by the color of their eyes what's going on, if you pay attention. You probably noticed that with Reko and some of the other Centauri here. Their eyes stop glowing when they're sick or very tired and they can get really pale, almost gray. But when they're upset or angry they go dark and the way they reflect light shifts. Takes a while to recognize but once you see it, it's clear. From what I heard the same is true for Delphians except their eyes don't glow. Never seen one close enough to check that out, though." She glanced at Coria. "This Arter's eyes didn't change the whole time. He's all bluster and that seems to be working for him."

Djari chuckled. "I think I could learn much from you, Sunshine."

Coria barked a short laugh.

Nova stepped closer to the woman. "You could, too," she said, keeping her voice barely above a whisper, tightly controlled to avoid the hissing sound that could draw attention as much as a shout. "See that Bellac rebel by the far window? And the one coming this way? Their rifles aren't charged. That means they either don't know what they're doing, which makes them dangerous because their side arms likely work just fine, or the Shri-Lan here are out of ammunition, which is just as interesting. Something else you should notice is that none of them are patrolling the hallway to the latrines, likely because they just don't want to. That tells me that they're a little short on discipline here. Also both dangerous and useful. Perhaps you could quit sniping at me and start paying a little attention to our options here. Sitting around and waiting for rescue isn't likely to work out too well for us. So let's damn well remember we're on the same side!"

Coria glared at Nova for an interminable moment as if working on some sort of retort. In the end, she simply gave Djari a long, meaningful look and stalked away.

Nova sighed and shook her head. "She doesn't get it."

"We all cope in our own ways, Nova," Djari said. "She's afraid. Everyone is. She'll come around. Hey, breakfast is served. Today's menu is a lovely clotted rice paste with at least three pieces of dried fruit. Accompanied by a cup of hot water that has once been in the same room with a tea leaf. My treat."

"Sounds lovely. I'll be there in a bit." Nova left him to hurry to the injured rebel whose bullets they had stolen yesterday evening. The woman was still dealing with her broken arm and had been left behind by her compatriots.

Nova knelt beside her pallet and checked the bruise on the woman's face. "How's the head," she said softly.

The Bellac groaned. "Like someone's hit me with a rock. Now that I think of it, that's probably what happened."

Nova gambled. "Arter said to get on your feet quick. I told him you're not going anywhere with that arm. He's got to chew on that."

"Thanks. Not much in the mood for getting shot at right now. Damn Air Command had a convoy of grunts brought in from Rim Station. Some general's taken over. Looks like there might be a ceasefire unless Arter gets in a mood. Which is likely."

This news gave Nova some hope. General Ausan led Air Command operations on Bellac and was not someone who would allow a siege to go on for long. "You think Arter's going to get desperate?"

"Don't know him that well."

Nova glanced around, trying to recall the name that the Caspian had used earlier. She lowered her voice to a conspiratorial tone. "Heard the furface say that Stoyan's outfit going to hit tonight."

"Good, about time. This is a lot of blood to give up for a damn prison. Pe Khoja better be worth all this. As diversions go, this is the biggest foul-up I could ever imagine."

"Can't imagine they'd leave a prison unguarded."

The woman made a scoffing sound. "Moshon ridge is hardly a prison."

"You get some rest. I'll send something to eat." Nova patted her shoulder, digesting this information to commit it to memory. The Moshon garrison at the ridge served as a holding area for captured rebels and local sympathizers. They were sorted, many of them let go, some turned over to Bellac authorities. If someone important was among them, perhaps unknown to Air Command, it would be the place to hit before he or she was transferred to Siolet's far more fortified prison.

She rose and hurried to where some of the workers sat around a shared bowl of food. She tugged on Djari's sleeve to pull him away from the others. Startled, he scooped up a plate of the rice mash and followed her to a less crowded spot.

"A private dinner," he said. "I like that." He handed her the plate when they had settled into their corner.

"We need to find out more about these rebels," she said, keeping her voice low. She ate quickly to avoid tasting the meal.

"What do you mean?"

"They must have supplies, food, equipment." She peered around him to ensure that no one was listening. A few of the guards had watched her talk with the rebel but now resumed their listless pacing along the perimeter of the hall. "I wonder if you can get some of the kids to scout around," she said, meaning the young Bellacs that were sent outside to fetch water and burn soiled bandages and other refuse. "Some of the slum rats are pretty savvy, from what I've seen. I'm sure the Shri-Lan are hoarding supplies for their leaders and whoever they feel is more important than this rabble."

He raised both eyebrows in surprise and with a hint of amusement. "You want us to steal from the rebels to help the rebels?"

She grinned. "Yeah. Though I need to get my hands on a transmitter. If they're talking to Command about the hostages, they will have stopped jamming com traffic. I'm guessing they're using the relays on the tether." She tapped the small metal triangle at her temple. "I can probably use this to get into their system and from there to Command."

"Sounds dangerous. Can I look?" He leaned closer to her and brushed a strand of her hair out of the way to study the device. Nova's first impulse was to shrink back but there was something wonderfully pleasant about his presence. Perhaps it was this special trait that made him such a skillful healer in the almost complete absence of any real training. She held still, drawing comfort from his closeness without bothering to explore why she felt that way. It had been a long time since someone had touched her this gently.

"Amazing," he said, so close to her ear that she felt the hair at her nape rise. "To think that this small interface can let you steer entire spaceships as you wish. It's almost magical." He drew away. "But then a brain is a magical thing, isn't it?"

She exhaled a little shakily and just nodded.

"Why don't you just use that as a transmitter? Or as a sort of homing beacon, anyway? There must be a way to track you with it."

"There is, but using these to transmit directly is too easily tapped. We'd be spotted by rebels at once. It's why we rarely use them wirelessly. But I can embed my ID code into a message using *their* transmitter and they won't know it's me."

"Why are you so set on sending a message? They must know where we are. They just have to figure out a way to get us while we're still alive."

"I overheard some things. All of this might just be a diversion to draw local Air Command troops here."

"Why?"

She pulled on her lower lip, thinking about that. "Just a feeling, really." She nudged his arm. "So do you think you can find us someone to look around? Nothing more. I'm not looking to get anyone into trouble. I just need to contact Command."

He nodded. "There's a delinquent or two that wouldn't mind sneaking around a bit. I think they've found the trick of getting around the Rhuwacs." He nudged his plate around on the floor. "I wish there was a way to get some of these other people out of here. Your friend Reko is not going to make it much longer and that Bellac with the chest wound won't either. They only have one lung."

"I'm sure someone's negotiating something. The explosions have stopped now."

"You have a lot of confidence in your people."

"Why wouldn't I?"

"Do you really think they care about a few civilians out here? For all we know, we're the only ones left."

"They'll worry about the outcome of not doing anything. As long as we're not yet allied with Bellac, the Union is going do all they can to avoid more casualties."

He smiled sadly. "That's it? Politics? And once Bellac has handed the planet over to you, would you walk away from these things? The rebels aren't going to leave us alone. Will you still be here?"

"Of course we will. We'll have a big stake in this place."

"The jumpsite."

"Well, yes."

"But not the people."

"Of course the people," Nova said, puzzled by his response. "We have bases wherever rebels are trying to take over. We'll keep the garrisons here on Bellac to protect you. And we're putting a monitoring station near the jumpsite to keep rebels out of your airspace."

"Wouldn't be necessary, would it, if there were no rebels."

"Now you sound like Coria."

He shrugged. "She has a point. You're only here because of the jumpsite. Those make it possible for your Union to expand, to travel to new places, to set up new trade. It's commercial. It's about wealth. And now so are the Shri-Lan."

"If they had any sort of organization they'd set up their own trade instead of trying to steal from others. There are other competitors of the Commonwealth and things work just fine with them."

"They're as tainted by rebels, criminals and pirates as your own groups are."

She frowned. "Who have you been listening to, my poet farmer friend? That's rebel propaganda you're getting into now."

"Is it?" He smiled. "And I thought I figured that all out by myself." He shook his head. "You control the jumpsites and that makes you very powerful. It's bound to create wars where us local poets get caught in the crossfire."

Nova nodded. He was right. A stable jumpsite inside a solar system ensured access to other worlds otherwise inaccessible via travel through real-space. The brief leap through subspace meant trade and migration for the people using it, and wealth for those who knew how to exploit it. The Union pounced quickly to include habitable planets like Bellac into the Commonwealth as soon as they were accessible.

The Union's military had not been an especially necessary organization until some of the locals rebelled against newly imposed rules and the changes that alien newcomers brought. Rebel groups merged into factions that slowly grew into a sizable opposition. Some, like the Shri-Lan, had members on many worlds, although lesser factions existed on almost all planets.

Over time, the powerful Shri-Lan had become an enemy force without a home planet and made up of any species that opposed Union presence. Funded through extortion, piracy and illegal trade in slaves, drugs, and weapons, they had established large territories not only on remote planets outside Union interests but also on vital worlds such as Magra and Pelion. Bellac had been in their sights when the Union finally escalated their negotiations for control of the planet.

And so pilots like Nova patrolled jumpsites and valuable installations, escorted transports, hunted down rebels, and defended settlements against enemy attacks. It had never occurred to her to question the rightness of doing any of this. The rebels were her job; their extinction her priority.

"It's the way we have to live now," she said. "Maybe we'll all have peace someday."

"At what price?" He pointed toward the untidy rows of pallets crowding the hall. "Look around, Lieutenant. Most of those people were maimed by your soldiers. Or got caught by missile strikes while trying to flee. Collateral damage is all we are."

Nova was surprised by the anger that had finally cracked the surface of his outward serenity. He had seen enough, done too much these past few days to hang on to his optimism and it pained her to see him in this state. She had to admit to herself that she had come to rely on him to infuse her with some of his tranquility.

"I don't pretend to understand all of it," she said softly. "And sometimes I wish we weren't so heavy-handed. But look. The Shri-Lan are using your people like shields; we often display our uniforms even when camouflage seems a lot more sensible. They recruit children and species barely able to comprehend what they're fighting for; we train our troops to treat our enemies humanely. We don't hold dying people hostage. We—" Nova interrupted herself with a sudden and peculiar awareness that her own words sounded like so much propaganda. She thought about Captain Beryl, as cruel and cold-blooded as any rebel. About Captain Dakad, quick to order the 'mitigation' of his downed pilot. Djari was right to worry about all of them being mitigated.

"Maybe we're not so noble, but given a choice I know on what side I stand."

"Do you have to be on any side?"

Nova hesitated. This was the second time someone had asked her to think about that recently. Only a day or two ago Reko had assumed she would leave Air Command at some point. Was it really that simple? "You'd have me stand by and do nothing? If I can help to defeat the Shri-Lan, why wouldn't I?"

He began to say something, paused, and then shrugged. "I suppose that makes sense. You're a warrior, Lieutenant Sunshine."

She smiled back at him, glad that he seemed willing to put this subject aside. "I am. And this warrior needs to stop being a nurse and get back to soldiering. Just don't tell Coria."

FIVE

"Are you sure you want to do this?" Nova whispered. "It'll be safer here for you."

Night and silence had fallen over the hall, interrupted only by the occasional moan from the injured and the murmurs of their guardians. A fan whirred somewhere in an attempt to stir the stifling and fetid air. Things had improved a little today with the arrival of another scanner and a handful of decon wands. More disinfectant was not to be found but they had received enough soap and fresh water to improve sanitation.

"I am," Djari said. "I'll be your lookout."

She retied the scarf around her head and then nudged Reko's legs to retrieve some of their concussion bullets. She transferred them to the pockets of the baggy trousers that now hid her own combat armor beneath it. Reko stirred with a groan but did not wake. She murmured soothingly and stroked his stubbled cheek. His fever had grown alarmingly and his wound was hot and swollen. They had tried to cool him down but there was little more than water for that. Nova thought of all the wonderful medical equipment available even out here, at the garrison near the other end of town, that would have him up on his feet and firing off his lame jokes within hours. Right now, it might as well be on the next planet.

"What are you going to do with those?" Djari asked.

"Just in case." She showed him the modifications Reko had made to the capsules. "Too noisy to use around here, but better than nothing if we find ourselves in a tight spot."

He untied a braided leather string he had been wearing around his neck, looped several times. He held it up to reveal a leather cup sewn into the middle, hidden under his hair. "We use these for hunting. I bet I can throw one of those things a long distance."

"Nice!" She examined the sling with appreciation. "And much safer, frankly. I throw like a little girl."

He laughed, a pleasant sound in the dark.

They looked up when Coria came with a bowl of water for Reko. She said nothing while she wiped his face and picked up some discarded bandages. Before she left, she looked from Djari to Nova, her gaze clearly conveying what her silence did not.

Nova watched her go. "She really doesn't like me."

"No, I don't suppose so."

"Why?"

He shook his head. "Doesn't like Humans. You seem to bother her especially."

Nova hesitated. "Is she your... I mean are you two..."

His teeth flashed in the dark when he smiled. "No. But she thinks I'm sweet on you."

Nova blinked. She had expected him to repeat Coria's fears that she was a risk to them, or perhaps even reveal that the woman was a rebel; something Nova had begun to suspect. "Um, what?"

He shrugged.

Nova tilted her head. "Is she right?"

"Subtlety is not your greatest gift, I think," he replied. "But I like that about you."

They waited for one of the rebel guards to wander past

them, his gun dangling lazily at his side. She nodded to Djari and they crept into a narrow hallway to the crude toilets that served the clinic. A service door leading to the septic area was only rarely inspected and quickly unlocked with a tool Nova had fashioned earlier. Clearly, their guards relied on the Rhuwacs patrolling outside to discourage escape attempts.

"Do the Rhuwacs have any weak spots?" Djari asked.

"Not really. They don't even feel pain. They don't see very well, but they can smell things going on in the next valley. Not much we can do about that."

Once through the exit, Nova paused and breathed deeply of the sweet, hot air outside the building. The sky was overcast but their eyes were already accustomed to the dark. She stopped Djari from slipping away and put a finger to her lips. Gradually, the night sounds around them became identifiable. A shuttle in the distance, possibly at the garrison. Some herd animals left behind by the fleeing population of Shon Gat. Muted voices far to the left. And, finally, the congested snuffling of Rhuwacs.

She flattened her hand high over her head before realizing that Djari would not know that to mean Rhuwac. But he nodded and held two fingers up for her to see. She agreed with his guess that there were two of them. She pointed away from the source of their sounds. Circling around them meant a delay in finding the shed their young scout had discovered. It also seemed a whole lot safer.

They moved silently. Djari's hunting experience served him well and she grew more confident in crossing the shadowed spaces in this warren of alleys and passageways. She counted the twists and turns until they reached the ancient wall that used to encircle the town before it had sprawled beyond its fortification. As reported, a metal shelter huddled among the whitewashed buildings, looking as out of place as any of the off-world constructions here. Light spilled from the open door and a lone Bellac sat on the stoop, busy with a pan of food.

Nova's eyes followed a rusted tower upward to see a net

of wires spread out from it, anchored to the nearby wall. A primitive array used by the Shri-Lan in remote areas, it provided excellent reception but was less effective for transmission. A lamp swung from the same mast, casting a bleak pool of light over the building.

She turned to Djari with a few gestures, cautioning him to remain here and hidden. He moved as if to object but she shook her head firmly. He scowled, obviously not convinced, but then nodded. She watched him fit one of the explosive charges into the sling and then turned her attention to the Bellac rebel.

Grateful for the long, drab vest that helped her blend into their surroundings, Nova sidled closer to the metal shed. There, she tested a plastic crate before stepping on it to peer into the dimly-lit interior. She made out some field equipment along the far wall where a woman slouched in her chair, feet on the cluttered bench. She was idly bending a length of wire into shapes while she monitored incoming messages that didn't appear to hold her interest. A rifle was placed just within reach on a cot beside her. The rest of the interior was crammed with crates and barrels, some of it arranged to form crude table and seats. Nova lowered herself back down and approached the front of the building.

The other rebel was still working on his dinner. Nova realized how hungry she was when the greasy chunk of bone and meat on his plate actually made her mouth water. She wrapped a long, thin string, made from a braid of sutures and medical tape, around her palms to form a garrote. With another quick glance around the alley, she stepped forward and used the choke to pull the rebel into the dust where his flailing legs made little noise. She felt the garrote cut deep into his throat, cutting off his shouts of fear and pain and, soon thereafter, his life.

Nova waited another minute, breathing harshly, alert to any sounds from the shed. She did not look at the rebel's face. As a pilot, she rarely faced her victims and she doubted that she could ever get conditioned to defeating them in close combat. It was best not to look, not to think about who these people were. Quickly, she searched him for weapons and came up with a sidearm laser, a decent knife and, oddly, a dart gun.

She raised her hand to prevent Djari from approaching. He was invisible in the but no doubt had been watching. She raised one finger and pointed toward the shack. The stoop creaked when she stepped on it.

"Hey, Jast," the woman inside called out. "Check this out. I should be an artist."

Nova stepped into the room and fired her new pistol at the back of the rebel's head. The stench of burned hair filled the room and she quickly went outside again to wave to Djari. She waited while he hurried to the hut. "Hide that body behind the shed," she said to him, pointing to the first rebel she had dropped. "Then sit here. Look like a rebel."

"What is all this?" he said, looking over the boxes behind her.

"Hopefully something useful. Oh, look!" She picked up a canvas bag that had caught her eye and handed it to him. "Med supplies."

Nova walked over to the console and pushed the rebel's chair out of the way before looking over the displays to tap into the com system. Random conversation dribbled from the speakers in sporadic bursts, none of it the sound of battle. Some expletive-laden exchanges among patrols, a more cerebral conversation regarding the hill villages, a lot of static.

She smiled when she spotted a portable perimeter scanner dangling in its case from a hook. "You know," she said to the lifeless rebel as she pulled the woman's data sleeve from her arm and a pistol from her belt. "If you'd watched your scanners instead of your art project you would have seen us coming." Grunting, Nova shifted the body to the floor and pushed it under the cot. It meant a small delay if someone came by here, but desertion was common among rebels and would be assumed before they'd start looking for bodies.

Nova connected her neural interface to the com system and entered a coded signal, barely a blip among the traffic. She waited. After a few seconds of peering out of the shack's grime-smeared windows, she sent another.

Finally, an answering signal came back to her from the base. She closed her eyes, concentrating on chatting in a bored, Feydan-accented voice about the miserable conditions out here and what she thought of Air Command. She carefully embedded, through code words and timed signals, the information about a possible prison break on the ridge and the name she had gleaned from the Caspian rebel. Whoever this Pe Khoja was, he was surely important enough to stage an assault against a guarded Air Command installation.

A hissing noise from the door caught her attention.

"Thought I heard something," Djari whispered when she came to stand behind him.

"Rhuwac, guessing by the size," she said after adjusting the scanner she had found. "Just one. Over that way. Let's get back to the clinic."

"Huh? Just shoot it."

"Ever try to lift a Rhuwac? We'll never get him hidden away. Besides, they smell, alive or dead. Those boxes are locked. Let's get out of here."

"Could be supplies in there."

She aimed her gun at a lock without using the tracer. It hit the spot, anyway, and the lock melted. "What's all this?" she said when the container revealed stacks of tightly packed tubes, coiled like some weird green sausage. She pried another box open and found the same.

"*Mince*," he said.

"What?" She turned her head to survey the stack of similar crates along the wall. "All this is dope?"

"Looks like it."

She sighed. At least this made some sort of sense. The demand for *mince*, a paste made from one of Bellac's succulent plants, was boundless in other parts of Trans-

Targon. The local, sturdy desert population enjoyed a chew of it as much as she might enjoy a glass of wine. Certain other species, notably Centauri and Feydans, achieved far more significant results with the drug, none of them healthy. *Mince* was extremely addictive. It was frowned upon in some places, illegal in others, and a very significant source of income for the Shri-Lan rebels.

"So that is what this is about? The reason why there are so many rebels in Shon Gat?"

"Been going on for years. Long before the Union even started to build the elevator. The stuff gets smuggled across the hills through Shon Gat and by caravan to the coast. Once it's on ships to Panyan they're in the clear. It's not illegal there. There are caches like this all over town. Some of the locals process it into other forms, too. Of course a lot of this gets smuggled off-planet as well. Your new garrison is complicating things."

"I had no idea. I suppose that's why everyone got so upset when Air Command started knocking on doors."

"Keeping you in the dark like a proper grunt, are they?"

She shrugged. "Just one more reason to rid this place of Shri-Lan. I don't care." She gave him a sheepish look. "Well, I do. Are they using the elevator for this?"

"Doubtful. Not with the kind of security you have. I mean, the elevator is standing right in the middle of your base. The caravans are a safer way to move this stuff. The governors are touchy about Air Command harassing the nomads." He lifted a length of mince from its box. "We'll take some of this. If we run out of pain meds for the Centauri at least we have this to get them through."

Both of them ducked for cover when the sharp rapport of a ballistic weapon cut through the night silence. Nova leaped from the doorway and pulled Djari into the shadows between two buildings, expecting rebels to return to this station. More gunfire racket reached them.

"Is that from the hospital?" Djari said. "Is that Air Command?"

Nova shook her head. "They wouldn't just blast in here at night. I'm not that important or they'd have done that already. Let's get closer."

A terrible roar rose up behind them, like something huge and angry and possibly in pain.

"Rhuwac," Nova said just as the creature ran at them from the alley. He was wielding a massive club in massive hands and Nova suddenly felt very very small. The brute shouted something about Humans and they saw spittle fly from between the slabs of teeth he bared. "Ugh," she said and aimed her weapon. It took a few passes from her gun before he fell, silenced.

Shouts reached their ears, closer than the gunfire still sounding in the distance. The Rhuwac's noise had alerted someone.

Djari stepped away from Nova and readied his sling. He let it swing a few times before it rotated around his wrist. At the correct moment he heaved back and let the projectile fly high into the sky. They heard it detonate in the distance, surely drawing attention for a while. As one, they turned and fled in the opposite direction, along the wall and into the slums.

They were breathless by the time they had put a safe distance between themselves and whatever was going on back there.

The door to one of the deserted homes did not yield to her pick but Djari forced it open with a few well-placed kicks below the lock. The single-room dwelling looked like whoever had lived here left in a hurry. Pieces of clothing and household items cluttered the floor and storage boxes stood open and empty. The corner used for cooking was cold. Djari poked around the looted shelves and found nothing edible.

Nova placed the scanner stolen from the rebel station onto a windowsill and found it in working order. There was no one nearby. "Safe here for a bit." Although there was still much interference from the rebels' jamming systems, she detected moving bodies throughout the quarter, many more than she had assumed to be here. Shots still rang out at intervals but the sound of voices and the ugly growl of Rhuwacs had faded away.

"What do you think happened?" Djari looked over her shoulder at the screen. "Are you sure those aren't soldiers?"

"Those guns are not military issue. I know the sound. Those are rebels. Maybe they noticed us gone." She winced. "Maybe they took that out on the others. Coria was right, perhaps."

"Don't think that way," he said. "There's nothing to be done about that now. That might not even have come from the hospital. We probably got turned around back here."

"Wish I could do that," she said dully.

"Do what?"

"Look at things the way you do. Don't you get scared?"

"Are you scared?"

She adjusted the display screen on the sill. "Of course I am. We're surrounded by rebels. Completely outnumbered."

"You do very well for someone who's scared. Not too scared to kill a man with your bare hands and a piece of string. Not too scared to shoot a Rhuwac like you're swatting a bug."

She lifted her shoulders slowly in a shrug. "That's just training. It kicks in. You must think that's all pretty awful."

"I do and it is. I could not do this… work. But being scared doesn't help things."

She turned to face him, suddenly aware that he was standing very close to her. His gray eyes were fixed on her own and there was a half smile on his dark face.

"You're scared right now?" he asked again.

She nodded.

"Wait a moment."

She frowned, mystified, but waited quietly for a long interval where only the sound of their breathing broke the silence.

"Now," he said at last. "Are you still scared?"

"Yes."

"So what good did it do you to be scared the first time I asked you? We're still in the same spot, with the same problem." He tipped his chin toward the town. "Be scared when you need to be. When it's actually useful."

"And when is it useful?"

He tapped a finger against her forehead. "When it keeps you from doing stupid things that'll get you killed. Good thing you have the training to keep up with your willingness to take risks, Lieutenant." His hand, roughened by work but gentle, moved to cup her chin.

Nova recoiled from his touch, her mind suddenly filled with a grim reminder of the last time a man had touched her that way. She stared at Djari's astonished face, momentarily and utterly disoriented, heart pounding.

"Nova?"

She shook her head to banish the memory, unable to recall what the head doctors at the base had told her to do with it. At the time it hadn't seemed so important to listen to their advice. "We have to keep moving," she said. "If we can scan them, they can see us, too." She snatched up the scanner and slung it over her shoulder. "If we keep moving they might think we're a rebel patrol. We need to get back there."

"Are you all right? I'm sorry if I... startled you."

She shook her head, wishing for nothing more than to go back a few seconds to feel his touch again. "No. You... you didn't. I'm sorry. Being silly. Jittery and tired."

"We should try to leave the town. Find a place to get some rest and then make our way around the foothills to your base. You can't go on like this. I'm barely able to stand on my feet, either."

"I have to see what's happened at the hospital. I won't leave Reko to them. Or the others. Coria doesn't much like me, but she's your friend. We have to try to help them now that we have some weapons." She pulled her gun from her belt and headed for the door.

"Nova."

She turned back again.

Djari took her arm to draw her close and this time she did not flinch when he bent to kiss her softly. He touched only her arms but Nova returned the kiss, letting the moment spin out deliciously to banish the hate-filled night from their minds, if only for a little while. More than that, she felt herself respond to the closeness of their bodies, of wanting him to touch her. The sudden and happy realization that this need had not been extinguished by Captain Beryl, after all, allowed her to reach up to wrap her arms around his neck.

But when she felt his hands on her waist to draw her closer to this powerful body she pulled away at once, the fear and memory a dash of cold water in her face. They stared at each other for uncounted moments, neither sure of the other.

He finally cocked his head and gave her a gentle smile. "Should I apologize?"

"Huh? No! I mean…"

He raised a single finger to point toward her. "Not going to shoot me, are you?"

She looked down to see that she now gripped her pistol close to her chest, one hand around the barrel, the other ready to engage the trigger. She exhaled forcefully and lowered the gun.

"This is what you look like scared," he observed. "But why?"

She looked away and then up into his face again, seeing only concern and curiosity. "I'm sorry. I… I got hurt, not so long ago. It's made me jumpy, I guess."

"Boyfriend trouble in the military? Is that allowed?"

She shook her head. "Not that. Not a boyfriend. I mean really hurt. On the base."

The soft smile faded from his lips. "On the base?"

She nodded.

He took a step closer, slowly as if worried that she might run away. He brushed her cheek with the tips of his fingers.

"You have nothing to fear from me," he said. "You know that, don't you?"

She nodded again and reached up to cover his hand with her own but then pulled away to open the door behind her. Perhaps there was time for this later, when she could allow herself to find out what his touch just now had meant. When she could admit to herself how much she needed it. She ground her teeth and shoved aside an overwhelming desire to hide in his embrace and, if even for just a little while, forget that she ever set foot on this planet. No time for any of this now.

"Let's walk slow so we don't look like we've got something to hide on the scanners," she said. "If we move fairly at random we could get close to the hospital without being noticed." She paused to reconsider. "Actually, let's not be seen by anyone. Ours or theirs. If they did send Union patrols they'll think we're rebels, too."

They made their way back to the edge of the slum along a meandering route until things finally began to look familiar to Djari who had spent far more time in these quarters than she had. But the Rhuwacs no longer loitered in the alley and no one else was moving nearby, according to her scanner. The hospital showed only a handful of life signs.

"No!" Djari exclaimed and she had to grasp his arm with both hands to keep him from rushing back into the building.

"Stop," she hissed. "We don't know who's in there."

He scowled at her but after a moment relaxed enough for her to let him go. She pulled him into the shelter of a courtyard wall and studied the dim glow of the scanner. This model only showed life signs but no specifics about species or state of health. At least they were alive. "Not moving. Could be our patients. Or people hiding." She pointed at the screen. "Is that the back area where we left Reko?"

"I think so. That's the hallway there, I think, given the exit."

She nodded. "Let's use the back door again. Just move very quietly. We're not helping anybody by walking in on rebels."

They stole around the side of the clinic and pried the door into the washroom. The floor was slippery with things she refused to examine more closely. No sound came from the main hall and power to the building seemed to have been cut. Feeling their way in the dark with an eye on the scanner, they crept forward to the nearest person.

It was, indeed, someone hiding. A Centauri woman, wrapped in a sheet from her bed, cowered in a corner.

"Shh," Nova whispered and touched her gently as she crouched beside her. "Are you hurt?"

The woman raised her tear-streaked face and looked from Nova to Djari, taking a moment to recognize them. "They shot them," she said. "All of them."

"Who?" Djari said. "What happened?"

"I don't know! They just came in here and started yelling and shooting. I ran and hid. They were shouting about the Union but no soldiers came. They just left." She stared blindly into the dark. "They just left."

"Stay here," Nova said. "Stay quiet."

Djari moved ahead of her around the corner and to the front entrance. They found another survivor, this one a Bellac worker, and then one of the locals that had supplied them with food these past few days. Nova pressed her hands over her face to stifle her cry when she saw a tall Centauri sprawled face down near the door.

"Gods, Reko," she moaned, although her scanner had already told them that none of the bodies strewn through the hall were alive. "Please, not this." She dropped to her knees beside him and heaved him onto his back. "Oh, damn!" She squeezed her eyes shut and dug her hands into his borrowed tunic as if to tear it.

"Come on!" Djari gripped her arm to pull her up. "We have to get out of here."

She shook him off. "I can't leave him here, in the dirt." The half-closed eyes in the dusty face seemed to accuse her of something. Why had she left him here, unable to defend himself? Now who would teach her to curse in Centauri? "I can't…"

"We have to. Let's go!"

"Djari," they heard a whisper. Coria came out of the shadows, uninjured but her eyes were wide with fear. "You're alive! Thank the Gods!" Djari held her tightly, his voice a soothing murmur, until she had collected herself. She seemed less excited to see Nova near him.

The three of them shifted Reko onto a pallet and covered him with a blanket. Their next priority was to collect the survivors and leave the hospital, more to escape the gruesome carnage than with any hope of finding a better hiding place. The alley outside was silent although they stopped and listened anxiously when some shouts reached them from afar. Another escapee huddled in a doorway of a looted and burned home and they convinced him to join them.

Coria led them to a small stable, smelling cleanly of hay and wood, where Nova arranged them along a rickety stairway to hide their true number on the sensors. She took stock. None of them were too injured to move on their own. The shell-shocked Centauri woman would have to be minded carefully. One of the Bellacs was little more than a child. The others just looked stunned and exhausted.

"What happened?" Nova asked Coria. She glanced guiltily at Djari. "Did they notice we left?"

"Then it's our blood on your hands, Human," Coria snapped.

"They did not," the Bellac medic said. "There is some sort of mutiny going on. Some of the rebels are trading captives to save their hides. Taking them out in the dark to bargain with. Thank the Gods they took the young ones out, first. Arter's people came and shot whoever's left, just to make a point. They shot their own, too."

"The rest are trying to get back into the hills," Coria said. "The ones who aren't turncoats."

Nova tapped her lips with a forefinger, considering this.

"Air Command is going to be all over those hills. Snipers are just going to pick them off. Surrendering is probably much healthier right now." She looked to Coria. "Do you know where and to whom they're delivering the hostages?"

The woman shook her head. "Guessing along the east side where it's more open."

"Going to be light soon," Nova said to Djari. "We need to get out of here. No guarantee we'll be found by the right sort of rebel."

"No, I suppose not. What do you have in mind?"

She looked up at the people on the stairs. "We're going to play Shri-Lan. I'll be your prisoner, and so will they." Nova pointed at the Centauri and a Bellac with a long gash across his cheek and a bandage around his head. "The rest of you look well enough to be rebels. We have a few guns." She turned away from them and pulled the data sleeve she had taken from the dead rebel from her pocket.

"Calling home?" Djari said and looked over her shoulder.

"Sort of." Nova frowned when the unsophisticated device balked at her manipulations. She managed to recode the access scan and then briefly touched the device to her neural implant.

Djari raised an eyebrow. "You can interface with that?"

"Not exactly, but I can create a recognizable signal. They'll know it's me."

"How?"

She shook her head. "You'd have to hold a gun to my head to find that out."

He frowned. "You don't trust me?"

She looked up, startled. "Of course I do. It's just not the sort of thing we talk about."

"Of course. I'm sorry."

"No need." She touched his hand and felt his fingers close around hers like the briefest of hugs. She turned back to the others. "Coria, you and… what's your name? Selvan? You two go back to the hospital and grab some clothes that look like something rebels would wear." She met the woman's eyes. "I'm sure you can figure that part out."

Coria looked as if some retort burned to be flung at Nova but then said nothing. She tugged on the medic's arm and they slipped back into the street.

* * *

There were nine of them now, making their way slowly along the outside of the old city wall toward the north end where Union patrols were sure to pick them up. The sun had risen not long ago, but a hot, dry wind already flapped their loose clothing and frayed their nerves.

Nova turned to walk backward for a moment, counting heads, before returning her eyes to the uneven terrain around them. She now wore her Air Command uniform and her hands were loosely tied behind her to appear as a hostage. It made walking on the uneven ground awkward and tiring.

A young man with a crutch hobbled beside her, slowing them all down, but he was a great story teller and managed to keep them distracted with his commentary. The Centauri woman had stopped talking long ago and continued moving only because Coria had tied a scarf around her wrist. Djari and the medic walked in the back, armed with the guns. The others surrounding them tried their best to look armed and menacing, a difficult feat for any of them as they stumbled along in the heat, not having eaten since the day before and with only a small bag of gritty water to sustain them. They stopped often to rest in what shade they found and each time they started out again it seemed more difficult to put one foot in front of the other.

They had met a small group of retreating rebels earlier. Their questionable disguise had worked or perhaps the rebels were too intent on fleeing into the hills to bother with challenging them. Feeling a little more confident, they continued their journey without having seen anyone else. The arid ground now sported considerably more scrub and the occasional tree, blocking the view from town and offering a little more shade.

She turned again, briefly, to look back at Djari. He looked up as if she had called to him and his tired face lit up with a smile. She remembered their moment together those few hours ago and the thought of another one like it, as his smile seemed to promise, gave her hope and renewed strength.

Nova glanced at Ulos, the young Centauri beside her. "Didn't anybody notice that he wasn't from around there?" she asked, referring to his latest, somewhat convoluted tale. Her head ached and she had trouble following the plot but it kept her from thinking about other things.

"That's the fun part. The difference between his markings and his lover's people are some loops across the left chest. So he used her paints to change his markings."

"He must have been truly in love," Nova said. Caspians prized few things as much as the intricate patterns on their short hide, a system that proclaimed their birthplace as precisely as a regional accent. Some females colored their hair to better display the patterns but males spurned the practice as effeminate. Neither men nor women would readily change the markings with which they were born. "So did they get found out?"

"Yeah," he said dryly. "He painted himself in front of a mirror."

Nova laughed.

They found an ancient wash-out and moved into the shade provided by the striated rock face of the gully. The ground sloped gently toward the north. "Let's hope it doesn't start raining," Ulos said. "A man could drown in here."

"Do not mention water."

He shrugged. "Would be salty, anyway."

"Someone coming," Coria said. She was holding the scanner. Interference was again reducing its range to just a short distance around them. "Four of them, that way."

Only a few moments later an armed rebel group traveling in the opposite direction came into view, hurrying to escape into the hills. Their guns were loosely pointed in their direction but they seemed to have no clear intent.

Nova's ragged column came to a halt when their way was blocked by the newcomers.

"Where would you be going?" A Centauri in a desert robe walked toward them. He stopped in front of Nova who kept her eyes on the ground and tried to look like a captive. It didn't take much pretension. "And where did you get the soldier?"

"Taking her back to *them*, what do you think?" Coria said.

The rebel shifted his eyes to her. "Arter broke off those useless talks. He said to scatter into the canyons. You're heading the wrong direction."

"To hell with Arter. We'll be scraped off the hills one by one as target practice. I'm getting out of here."

"You might want to rethink that, Bellac," he said. Nova groaned inwardly at their sad luck of having run into a rebel actually loyal to this lost cause. The man stabbed his gun into Nova's midriff. "I think we'll be taking her off your hands."

Just then a row of armed Union soldiers rose up on the embankment above them, appearing out of nowhere. No one had noticed their silent approach, too worried about the rebels coming their way. Confused, all of them looked around to face a wall of muscle in battle gear.

"Away from her," one of them ordered.

Nova gasped when she recognized Captain Beryl, not monitoring his squad, but himself behind the barrel of his gun.

The leader of the newcomers whipped around, gun ready, and was immediately met by a storm of laser fire. Others, too, fell to their aim and Nova saw Coria collapse and then Ulos also dropped before she managed to tear herself out of her shock. She pulled apart the loose knot that tied her hands and waved frantically.

"Stop! Cease fire!" she shouted, not daring to move into the crossfire. "Stop! Civilians!"

They stopped, but her companions lay dead or dying on the ground. She turned to find Djari still on his feet but with an arm scorched from wrist to elbow. Another burn had blistered the side of his handsome face. He stared at the bodies on the ground and stumbled back, shaking his head in disbelief. She took a few steps toward him but someone gripped her arm.

"Djari!" she cried, but the look he gave her felt like an accusation. He lurched away to flee into the scrubby hillside. When one of the soldiers aimed to fire after him, Nova pushed the gun aside to let the shot go wild. "That's not a rebel!"

She turned and launched herself at Beryl, gaining speed over the short distance to hit his chest with outstretched arms. "You fucking bastard!" He stumbled back, utterly surprised by her attack, and fell over a rock beside the path. She landed on top of him and smashed her fists into his face, cursing, unaware of the tears that poured over her face, unable to stop even when blood gushed from his nose and lips. "You. Fucking. Bastard!" she yelled again and finally someone pulled her away, needing another soldier's help to keep her from returning to cause more damage.

Nova struggled with the men, too enraged to give up her insane desire to murder the captain, a man more than twice her size. He struggled to his feet, wiping at his streaming face.

"Look what you did, you stupid bitch," one of his men said. "What the hell was that about?"

Beryl explored a gash across his eyebrow and then looked at his blood-covered hands. "Let her go," he said.

"Captain?"

"You fucking heard me."

Nova nearly fell when the soldier released her with an angry shove. She breathed in sobbing gasps, her hands on her knees, furious and exhausted. "Those are civilians trying to get me out of this place. Why did you open fire? Look at this!"

"He raised his weapon," Beryl said and then seemed to realize that he sounded defensive. "As far as we saw, they were rebels. Our orders are to retrieve you. Now get your ass in motion and back to base."

"I'm done taking orders from you," she said and paid no attention to the looks of astonishment among his men. She knelt beside the unconscious Coria. "We're taking her with us. And anyone else who's still alive." She glared at Beryl. "Do you get that?"

He grasped the back of her suit and hauled her to her feet. "You are pushing your luck," he said. "We'll just assume you've lost your fucking mind." He turned to his men. "Grell. Silas. Double-time to the gate and bring an evac back here."

* * *

The hours that followed passed like a feverish dream. Too weak to continue the trek to the base, Nova was made to sit in the shade while the soldiers stood guard. She did not recall talking to any of them or seeing Beryl after this. Someone eventually pulled up with a skimmer and the few survivors of this latest massacre were taken away.

The medics at the base received her, someone propped her up while she took a long shower and then she was tucked into a cot in the garrison's well-equipped hospital compound. Coria was also there, asleep or unconscious, and an armed guard stood by the tent entrance. Nova was treated for dehydration and finally allowed to sleep before she remembered to ask why they had posted the guard.

The following day brought a bedside debrief. And another, conducted by someone else. She talked about Sergeant Reko and Arter and the conditions at the crude med station near the slums. She tried to recall the location of the anti-aircraft guns they had seen in the hills and that still hadn't been found. She asked about Coria, who was no longer in the hospital tent, and was not given an answer. Then she was left alone again, feeling restless and ready to leave this place.

At the end of that day several officers entered the tent. She sat up and put her feet on the floor as did two of the more able patients that shared her space.

"At ease," they were told as the general approached.

"Yessir," Nova said, not at all at ease to be sitting here in a hospital gown while General Patrina Ausan stood before her. The Centauri, who once spoke at the flight academy on Magra while Nova was still a greenie, had been an inspiration for her since her image first appeared on the massive overhead screen of the lecture hall. Now she was leading Air Command's primary base on the other side of Bellac Tau, making the new skyranch her responsibility. Nova had to remind herself to stop gawking at the woman.

"I heard you were still lazing around, Lieutenant."

"I… um what?" Nova stammered.

The general surprised her by sitting on the edge of the cot. Her glossy black hair was tightly bound and the uniform more crisp than any fabric had the right to be in this weather. Nova wondered, not for the first time, how senior officers managed this. "I'd say it's well deserved," Ausan said. "How are you feeling?"

Nova blinked up at an adjutant waiting by the door and then back at the general. "I'm recovered. I wasn't injured. Just exhausted. Ready to return to duty, General."

"We'll let the doctors decide that, Whiteside. I want to commend you for your warning about the attack on the ridge. We got reinforcements out there just in time. And you were correct. One of the captives there turned out to be a very important Arawaj rebel, most notable for the fact that he's working directly for Tharron himself."

Nova whistled. Tharron's position as the absolute leader of the Shri-Lan made him Air Command's most desired target. "Thank you, General. I'm glad I was able to help. I'm afraid not much else went according to plan back there."

"Yes, well, we cannot gleefully call this a victory. The militants have been routed from Shon Gat and the hill villages but the price was too steep." The Centauri stood up again. "You'll return to your base in the morning. When you've been declared fit you'll rejoin your squad and head for the jumpsite." She smiled. "I think we can use someone with your resourcefulness up there."

Nova was certain that the broad grin that spread over her face made her look just a bit foolish. "Thank you, General." She bit her lip. "May I... may I ask, um..."

The officer raised an eyebrow.

"There was someone, a Human, who helped us. At the hospital. When we went out to send the message. And later, when we escaped. He was lost. And injured. I wonder what became of him."

"What is his name?"

"Nathon something Djari. Goes by Djari. He's applied to work on the skyranch so we probably have a record of him here."

Ausan's lip twitched in amusement. "And you'd like to see him make his way there?"

"Well, yes. But mainly I'm just worried about how he's doing."

The Centauri nodded to her aide who got busy with his data sleeve. "We'll see what we can find. You just get rested up, Lieutenant."

"Yessir." Nova watched the general leave through the tent flap held aside for her and then nearly collide with a soldier trying to enter. He stood aside and saluted as she passed him without comment.

"Gods, Rander, you idiot," Nova said. "You almost knocked her over."

The sergeant looked over his shoulder and shrugged. "I don't think Lady Patrina is so easily knocked over." He flopped onto her cot far more casually than their commander had just done. "How come you rate your own bedside general?" He gave her a bowl of pudding filched from the mess hall.

She accepted the bowl and decided not to scold him for scattering dust over her sheets. She had recently become very fond of clean bedding. "Congratulating me, I guess. No one even told me why she's out here."

"Mopping up this mess, of course. Plus she found out that Major Trakkas is shuffling his pilots to places they have no business being and I think that irked her plenty. I hear she almost had his stripes when she heard you were MIA. Misplacing a pilot is a bit of a problem, I guess. You people are expensive."

"Is that why he sent that commando after me? With Beryl at the helm?"

"Yah. They caught your signal. Nothing more fun for Beryl's bunch than tracking rebels. Must have been a party for them. They never seem to get prisoners back in one piece. Going to finish that?"

"Yes. Hands off." Nova savored the sweet treat. "Sending Beryl must seem amusing to him."

"To Major Trakkas? Why?"

Nova shrugged. "Long story."

"Give me some gossip, Loot! I heard you punched him out."

"You guys are like little old ladies. I barely touched him." Nova stared into her pudding. No one had mentioned her attack on Captain Beryl. No one had asked about the death of those civilians. Collateral damage in shades of gray where both of them had stepped over the line. A matter best left in the dark, perhaps.

Sergeant Rander reached over to nudge her hand, bandaged where the skin of her knuckles had split on Beryl's teeth. "He got sent out with his squad, but when I saw him his face was a shiny purple mush. An improvement, some say."

She shook her head to push the memory aside. "I'm out of here, too. Guess I'm getting my plane back, finally. The general said we're heading up to guard the jumpsite. I can't wait to get off this rock and back out into space." She set the empty bowl on a table beside her cot. "I'm sorry about Reko. Tell the others he did his job. There wasn't any way he could have avoided getting shot."

Rander winced. "Yeah, I know. We were briefed. He was

a good soldier. We lost thirty-two troops, plus Beamer's unit in the hills. Almost two hundred civilians. As many shipped off to hospitals. Could have been worse, I guess."

"Could have been better, too."

SIX

"This is the fourth time I've brought this ship in here and you people ask me the same thing every single time. It gets tiresome."

Nova kept her eyes on the cockpit data display scrolling a list of the new arrival's inventory. Her scanners reported a shipment of foodstuffs not found on Bellac Tau along with barrels of liquor from Feyd and what scanned like bales of fabrics, possibly clothing. There were also about a dozen passengers in one of the cabins of the transport they had waylaid as it emerged from the jumpsite. Her findings were confirmed by the sensors of Lieutenant Rolyn's Kite on the other side of the ship.

"Yes, sir," she said.

"You know I have to go through all this at customs," the captain of the trader complained.

"Your destination is Siolet, then?" Nova entered the name of Bellac Tau's largest city into her system. Besides housing the Union's main base there, it was also its primary trade hub. "Not the skyranch?"

"You know damn well I'm going to Siolet! Why don't you go chase rebels instead of bothering traders?"

"Rebel activity has increased in this sub-sector, sir. Your safety is our primary concern. Do you require an escort to the planet?"

"Your rebels aren't going to chase me for my dresses. I told you I'm going to Siolet. I don't need you to follow me to make sure of that."

Her shift partner cut in, unheard by the civilian. "You're so polite, Whiteside. He's going to pop a vein for sure."

She grinned. "Anything on voice?"

"Yeah. Human. Not so much irritated as scared spitless. Spiking all over the place. Can't see what he's hiding in there, though. Those could be slaves."

"Let Ground handle this one." Nova returned her attention to the trader. "It's no trouble at all, sir. We're glad to help you arrive safely." She watched Lieutenant Sool pull forward and take up position beside the transport ship, ready to escort it to the surface. "We wish you and your crew a very pleasant stay on Bellac Tau."

Nova closed the com link and sent their findings to the Air Command carrier hovering not far from the jumpsite. Their squadron had patrolled this area for fifty of Bellac's short days in anticipation of saboteurs that might have dodged patrols on the other side. The Union relay station near the jumpsite, like the skyranch also still under construction, made an attractive target. Once it was guarded by a permanent Air Command detail, the squadrons would leave for their next assignment.

"You're a wicked woman, Whiteside," Rolyn said.

Nova signaled him to return to the jumpsite to join the rest of their flight and await the next arrival. "We were told to be courteous, weren't we? Been a quiet day, sort of. I like that."

"Since when?"

Besides a shipment from Targon of materials for the unfinished relay, they had monitored just five arrivals during their shift. Three had exchanged polite conversation with the tedious but necessary Air Command checkpoint, one had tried to bribe them and was tagged as smuggler but harmless, and this was the only one today to complain about Union presence here. Predictably, it also seemed to be the one with the most to hide.

To traverse these instant subspace connections between far-flung sectors required powerful shields and even more powerful processors. Commonly, massive transport fleets provided berths to lighter vessels for the passage. It made for crowded ships and chaotic inventories. The liners, meant for migration and trade, often smuggled rebels between sectors and presented the greatest challenge to Air Command patrols.

"Black sky cruiser coming in from Bellac," they heard Lieutenant Sulean's voice. "Origin Panyan. In a hurry."

"Panyan, eh?" Heiko Boker cut in. "Not a lot of traffic coming out of that continent. Is this something new?"

"Negative. No air fields in that jungle. Looks like our visitor took a round trip to hide home base. Piece of junk. Strange configuration."

"Your turn to get the story, Heiko," Nova said.

Boker and his wingman moved to intercept the new arrival. Nova scanned the ship while he made his respectful inquiries. "Surprised that thing made it this far," she said over a closed band. "But fully shielded. I can't even get a good look inside. Want to bet it's carrying something it doesn't want us to see? Might want to get your fangs out, Boker."

The squad moved into a slightly more aggressive formation as the cruiser approached the jumpsite without slowing as was expected in this area.

"Well, he's not talking to us," Boker said after repeating his request for identification. "Tower?"

"We've notified Siolet," came the reply from the carrier. "Do not engage. Stand by."

"I feel they are lacking respect and common good manners," Boker grumbled but stood down to let the cruiser pass. Without permission from Bellac's governors none of them had the authority to waylay a traveler unless they were met with hostility. And until the construction was complete and the skyranch and elevator operational, Air Command had no authority to shut down the jumpsite's guide beacons.

"What did I just see?" Rolyn yelled.

The others, too, took a moment to realize that the large cruiser had disengaged two smaller ships, no bigger than the Kites themselves. The main body veered and headed for the jumpsite's relay construction, firing as it approached on a collision course. The separated components streaked toward the jumpsite itself.

"It's going to ram the relay," the Air Boss transmitted. "We've got this. Engage the two bogeys."

Nova whipped her Kite around and raced after the escaping ships.

"Beacons are responding. Jumpsite is opening," Boker said. "I'm right behind you, Whiteside."

Indeed, their systems warned them that someone aboard the fleeing ships had tapped into the beacons that allowed navigators to enter subspace. The site opened, soon large enough to allow them to enter.

"Who the hell's aboard this thing? What fucking nerve!" Boker yelled. He fired into the lead ship's shields. The other plane, not busy with opening this gateway to Magra, returned his fire and kept all of them dodging and weaving in their wake.

"Going in," Nova said.

"Shit," Rolyn replied. They were all aware of his aversion to traveling through subspace. It was a common phobia, even among pilots.

"Stay here, Rolyn," they now heard Captain Dakad from the carrier. "Boker, Sulean, Nieri, Whiteside. Go."

Nova set her course to follow the lead ship into the breach at ever-increasing velocity, letting them use up their coolants to calculate the passage. Sulean's guns streaked past her and the second ship spun away, disabled. "Nice shot, we're going—"

Nova's remaining words were only in her head. They had passed the threshold into the 'Big Empty' and hurtled into the frightening nothing-void of subspace. She saw nothing, or at least there was nothing that her brain seemed to recognize any more. Felt nothing. Heard nothing. She was unable to move and only her thoughts felt alive, reaching a panic state that, for some, could cause lasting damage during a long jump.

This was not a long jump and the breach soon spewed the ships back out into real space to scramble for bearings. Nova's neural interface grappled for the momentarily disrupted controls and she wasted no time in scanning for their quarry. It was also tumbling through space ahead of them and, as she watched, steadied and changed course.

"Battle cruiser ahead!" Boker called.

"I see it," Nieri said. "Probably thought we'd take the carrier through instead of the Kites. Damn."

"We've got time," Nova said. She reached for her console to override the power management system.

"Time to get roasted, maybe," Sulean answered. "We're in range. *Their* range."

"Whiteside…" Nieri began.

Nova punched every bit of power into her Kite, shortcutting a few routines via her interface to coax more speed from her plane. It raced ahead of the others, pushing the limits of the machine to bring the enemy fighter into her gun sights.

"Should have just said hello when we asked, assbucket!" Boker chortled when her guns took the ship down. "Uh oh." The cruiser had issued a swarm of Shrills in retaliation, looking like angry insects around a hive.

"Out of here!" Nova shouted and then held her breath while her Kite seemed to make the turn back to the jumpsite far too slowly. The other three Union pilots fired past her to hold back the enemy ships as she raced toward the jumpsite. "Going negative," she warned as the first to arrive there. She signaled the beacons and began to feed energy forward to create the opening.

"Remind me, Whiteside, you do have your chartjumper creds, right?" Sulean asked, somewhat nervously.

She did not reply, too focused on the mental connection with her plane. Once again, they plunged into the breach, losing all senses until they had crossed the unimaginable distance between Magra and Bellac Tau.

The other ships awaiting them veered out of the way to let the four Kites right themselves.

"Might be some Shrills coming through, team," Nieri said, unruffled by any of this. "Do we still have a relay?"

"Everyone's accounted for, Lieutenant," the Air Boss transmitted. "That delivery didn't make it. Salvage team is on the way. Return to base, Sulean. You're reading a little jittery. Status, Nieri."

"Enemy battle cruiser over there," the pilot said. "Complement unknown. We took down the bogey. Whiteside's probably a little short on coolant."

"Heard. We'll alert Magra. Resume patrol pattern. We'll send replacements early."

The squad hovered around the jumpsite, waiting for any sign that it might be opening to admit the enemy Shrills, perhaps even the battle cruiser, into Bellac space. It didn't happen. Whoever had awaited the two rebels over there had decided to cut their losses.

"Too scared to come over here with their fancy cruiser and engage properly," Nieri guessed.

"Just think," Boker said, sounding meditative. "We were almost home there for about a minute or two. Hard to imagine."

"Where's home, Heiko?" Nova asked.

"Got family on Zera. And here I am, back on the other side of Trans-Targon again. Should have dropped by to say hello."

She chuckled. "It's another jump from Magra to that subsector. And about five days in real space between jumpsites to get there."

"Well, still closer than this blip on the map."

"Where's home for you, Nova?" Rolyn asked.

She looked up from her controls and out into space. "Right now right here, I guess."

"Oh," he said. "Well…"

An hour later a trader came through, somewhat startled by the squad's battle-ready formation, to inform them that there was no one near the jumpsite terminus on the other side.

"Boys and girl, our relief is here," Boker announced not long after that. "Gather round, another busy, busy day in the service of our glorious Commonwealth Union is about to conclude with a considerable imbibement of glorious grain spirits personally smuggled from Bellac by your role model, Lieutenant Heiko Boker."

"You are such a drunk, Boker," Nova said and moved to formation.

"Role model for my pet churry, maybe," another pilot said.

"Imbibement-whatever you said isn't even a word," Rolyn added.

"Don't grief me, Rolie," Boker shouted. "We're on the brink of three days' worth of downtime. Admire my stupendous splendicity or I'll go to Siolet without you."

"Nice work, Rolie!" Nova said. "Three days having your quarters all to yourself."

"Wait a minute…" Boker said.

"This chase was combat level," Lieutenant Nieri interrupted. "What's your count now, Whiteside?"

"This little jaunt's going to buy me four points, at least," Nova said. So far, out here, she had not accumulated many of the type of flight hours recognized for her Hunter Class minimum. For the most part, they had cruised around, mindful of Captain Dakad's complaints about wasting fuel, and harassed the tourists. She needed documented precision flying or combat hours to qualify.

"Five if I'm lucky." Jumping a Kite through subspace,

even just via a charted breach, certainly counted. "We need to start a brawl like this every day."

"Why five?"

"Depends on Dakad's mood," Boker supplied. He drawled his words as if that somehow made him sound more like a Centauri. "If he says: 'That was damn bold, Whiteside, good job,' she's got the point. If he starts yelling about chasing bogeys *toward* an enemy battle cruiser stuffed with Shrills she can forget about it."

The last of the Kites, except for Lieutenant Sool currently on his way to the surface with the disgruntled would-be smuggler, had joined formation and they now swooped past their arriving replacements to head back to the carrier.

Nova was not particularly eager for time off. She did not care to join the others in whatever carousing they had in mind for their time in the capital. There was nothing for her at the base and remaining aboard the carrier just meant that someone would surely find work for her to do. She listened silently to her squadron mates' artless banter while they slipped their Kites into the carrier's narrow chutes to be turned over to the hangar crew.

The daily debrief was of course focused on the mysterious and, as usual, random rebel attack on the relay. Reports about the battle cruiser in the Magran sub-sector had not yet arrived. Nova pulled her head between her shoulders when her Kite's recordings of the last part of the chase were displayed. Captain Dakad pinned Boker with a violet glower when he said, "Good job, Whiteside." Rolyn gave her a congratulatory punch on the shoulder.

Finally, Dakad held up a hand when the pilots started to shift in their seats, expecting dismissal. "One more thing," he said. "We're a go for rotation. We'll transfer to the skyranch for a couple of sets so you can get familiar with the place. Have your quarters cleared before downtime – we'll be billeted on the orbiter." He looked meaningfully at some of his men. "I want those cabins left spotless. I want you ready to clear out the moment we dock. What you do then with your downtime is up to you. You can take the shuttle to Siolet or stay on the skyranch."

"Yesss," Nova whispered happily. Although the orbiter was still very much under construction, she had been eager for a chance to look around. No doubt some of the others were also rethinking their plans. Her memories of a few years spent on a skyranch were happy ones. Routines and rules were less stringent than those on the bases where she had lived and she had found friends among the other children. Somehow there had always been something to do between the lessons and chores designed to keep them all out of trouble.

She also looked forward to joining up with Caga squad, part of her wing and already stationed at the skyranch. Unlike her own, that squadron included female pilots and Nova anticipated gentler company, perhaps even an interesting roommate.

But something else was foremost on her mind. Had Djari made it up to the ranch? During these past few weeks of duty aboard the carrier, she had heard nothing more about him or any of the others that had survived the Shon Gat siege. Memories of that one sweet moment they had shared kept returning to her but when she recalled his face she saw only the reproachful look he had given her before he disappeared.

She had been tempted to make inquiries or to pull up personnel files but then decided against it. Looking up a fellow captive of the Shon Gat siege might just catch the attention of her counselors who still monitored her post-trauma state.

Dakad tugged on his nose, something he did when putting his words together. "Whiteside. Stay a moment. The rest of you are dismissed."

The others filed out, not without throwing a few curious glances in Nova's direction. Boker rolled his eyes and gave her a smile meant to encourage. Dakad rarely dealt with his pilots individually. It was often a sign of trouble.

The captain tipped his head toward the exit and waited for her to get up and join him. Puzzled, she walked with him around the clearance of the landing chutes and then into the interior corridor of the carrier. "Whiteside, I want to give you some notice about the rotation to the skyranch," he said finally.

"Sir?"

"We've had noise about rebel movements and there was some evidence found to assume sabotage attempts on the station."

"I'm aware, sir."

"General Ausan decided to provide Skyranch Twelve with additional security units. In fact, she's rotating the current skyranch and elevator security personnel to the base and vice versa to give everyone a change of scenery."

Nova winced. "Major Trakkas is coming up here?"

"No. He's going to command the garrison at the elevator base. The skyranch is commanded by Lieutenant Colonel Thedris until we turn it over, so we'll be working under him. We'll make the announcement tomorrow."

"I don't suppose Major Trakkas is very happy about that." Nova peered up at him, suddenly realizing why he was telling her this now. "Ausan transferred the ground units up, too, didn't she? Beryl and his thugs."

"Yes. She doesn't want to use pilots where ground pounders will do. They're providing security around the loading docks up there. Patrolling the construction sites. They've been there a while and I wanted to give you some warning. I don't have to tell you…" he trailed off, waiting for her to fill in missing words.

Nova stopped walking. "To keep my door closed? To make no trouble? Not hit him, maybe?"

"No. I won't do that. I am giving you the option to transfer to Zenta squad flying out of Siolet if you prefer. No one will think less of you for that, Lieutenant."

"I'm not running from him," she said at once.

"Think about it."

They continued to walk toward the officers' quarters. His offer, made in private, seemed sincere. It would mean less tension among his pilots if she transferred and it would certainly be a relief for her. Perhaps one of her well-meaning counselors had even suggested it. Still, hiding from Beryl was utterly unacceptable to her. It felt like running away.

"No," she said. "I will stay with my squad." She hesitated, needing to know. His ire over her decision would tip the scales here. Did he really think of her as so fragile? Perhaps punching Beryl had not been the best way to display self-control and fortitude under pressure. "What is your preference, sir?"

He did not look at her. "You're a fine pilot, Whiteside. You have the grit. The men respect you and that's where it counts. You will make Hunter Class and that looks good on me, too." He allowed himself a faint smile. "I see no reason for you to transfer."

Nova kept her expression carefully neutral. "Thank you, sir."

"I also think you can work out your issues with him here. Deal with it. You don't have to interact. I can try to get his gang scattered a bit. But anything more would require explanations to our new CO and perhaps even the general. And that will raise questions about the reporting by both you and Major Trakkas."

"That won't be necessary." Nova had heard the note of disapproval in his comment about the reports. She wanted to ask him, but then decided not to press him about it. "Thank you for giving me the option."

He gave a curt nod and opened the door to his quarters. "Whiteside," he called her back when she continued along the hall. She turned. "I'm pleased by your decision. I think maybe I was wrong about you."

* * *

"Now *this* is what this entire place is all about." A Centauri officer waited for her small gaggle of sightseers to gather on the catwalk overlooking the elevator hub. Skyranch Twelve was not designed to attract much of a tourist crowd, unlike the ones above the ice-bound Feron where few inhabitants had ever seen food grow above ground or Feyd where a thick atmosphere made launching into space from an orbiting platform far more affordable.

The two orbiters that would serve Bellac were designed purely for the manufacture of food and electricity and down here, on the lowest level where the tether from the ground met the station, things were pretty much utilitarian. Nova had expected a modern passenger handling area, perhaps kiosks where one could get more information about the tether's nanotube construction, or a spot to take some video of the planet hanging over their heads.

Instead, the area they were now shown looked like any loading dock she had ever seen on any base station or transport ship, albeit much larger. Metal floors and walls, cold metal railings, hoists, trolleys, storage containers and control stations. Workers bustled in the clear space around the tether to prepare for a new arrival from the ground. Nova's group leaned over the railing to watch, restricted from entering the steady, well-ordered routines on the floor.

"Hard to believe, isn't it?" Boker propped his elbows on the metal bar. After Lieutenant Rolyn had decided to abandon him in favor of the skyranch, Boker had given up his plans for Siolet's alehouses. Besides, the orbiter had two very nicely stocked lounges. His eyes traveled upward along the cable. "Look how thin that tether is. You don't notice that down on the ground."

Nova nodded. Their temporary guide chatted about tensile strength, payloads and velocity while actually holding a cross section of the nanotube belt in her hands. On the ground, near Shon Gat, the bottom part of the elevator was protected by graphene cages as well as shielding. As support for a system of sensors, com gear and defensive measures, its width seemed far more reassuring than this ribbon. Maybe the extra girth near the ground was intended to keep passengers from fleeing in terror. "I think I might be too scared to go for a ride down this thing," she said. "The skyranches I've been to weren't tethered."

"Imagine sitting in a box tied to this for three days."

Nova turned to the guide who had stopped to take a breath. "Will this be used for passengers?"

"Not at this time. It just takes too long. Once we're fully staffed, the station will operate a commuter shuttle for round trips every twenty days. We'll have emergency vehicles, of course, and a private transport company is going to offer trips to the surface if you can't wait for the shuttle. So far we have just cargo pods traveling along the tether. Eventually we may bring in a passenger car for those who want the experience of traveling through space that way. It's not a priority for Bellac."

A slight vibration ran through the metal plates on which they stood and then a massive climber descended from the ceiling. Those among the pilots who had not seen a climber at the Shon Gat base gasped in awe at the sheer size of it, looking like a small transport ship sliding down along the tether. Nova had expected rollers and cables or perhaps magnets but the assembly attaching the climber to the elevator reminded her of one of the frustrating engineering puzzles at the academy. The cargo bins, once released by the protective shielding, slid effortlessly onto tracks leading into the adjacent holding area.

"Not a box, then," Boker said. "Might actually be fun."

"I prefer to be in charge of steering whatever is hauling me through space," Nova replied.

"The elevator is of course powered by solar energy," their guide gestured downward although from here they were unable to see the transparent dome on the other end of the station, surrounded by vast arrays of solar panels and communication systems. "But we also use the regenerative braking power of the downward crawler to power the upward movement." She smiled. "Of course, up and down is a matter of opinion. Halfway there, gravity plays a big part no matter which way you go. And since the station's gravity spinners are now below us, the planet is actually above our heads. We are, from Bellac's point of view, upside down."

Nova watched the dock hands unload the container. "What's all that?"

"Supplies for the station, water, gasses. Much of that will of course be manufactured right up here eventually but we still have a lot to do before the farm rings are producing. We also accept shipments of export goods. Beyond those doors are air locks able to accommodate five transports at a time. The freighter leaving from there is taking those barrels of *anai* oil into Trans-Targon. It's worth a lot there. So by acting as a shipping port, the station is already starting to pay for itself because those shippers don't need to land in the atmosphere. Currently, we see one of these transports once every few rotations, but eventually the traffic will be constant."

"That's a lot of *anai* oil," Boker said. He bent far over the railing to look over the rows of shipping containers waiting to be handled. Nova resisted an impulse to grab the back of his jacket to keep him from going over.

"Bellac also exports frozen seafood that your people eat in huge amounts, Lieutenant. Skyranch Thirteen will be at sea and include a sub-surface processing plant. By using the ranches for most of Bellac's import and export activities, we should be able to curtail the smuggling of *mince* and exotics."

"Drugs and slaves," Boker translated out of the side of his mouth. Nova boxed him lightly in the ribs.

Their guide had heard him. "Unfortunately that is true, Lieutenant. The demand for *mince* outside Bellac is increasing. Fortunately, so far no one has tried to smuggle slaves using the elevator. We have, however, confiscated animals in stasis destined for the pet trade, a horrible practice and of course a violation of other planets' ecosystem management policies."

"Huge demand for churries on Targon," Boker said wisely. Some of the others snickered.

"What about security here on the platform?" Nova asked.

The officer pointed around the domed hall, probably glad for the change of subject. "This area is normally restricted to all but transport personnel. We've got video surveillance, armed guards on all levels, and this access area to the tether can be closed off from the station in a matter of seconds. Air Command presence here will depend on current threat levels. The tether itself is shielded in ways that I can't tell even you, Lieutenant, and of course the cargo bins are shielded individually against radiation and temperature fluctuations on the way to and from the planet."

"She probably doesn't know, either," Boker mumbled behind his hand as they dutifully trotted after their host and out of the shipping area.

"Expect some gravity shifts," she advised as walked along a curving passage. "We are going to walk around the gravity generators on our way to the upper levels. If you use the lifts this will hardly be noticeable. They move horizontally as well as vertically. Of course, you won't have much need to come down this way."

They soon reached a broad observation level that allowed a view of the exterior of the orbiter as well as an overlook into the hollow interior space. They were able to step out onto the bowed wall and, as pilots and inured to vertigo, all of them took that opportunity to look down into a central recreational area and then up to see the massive skylight. The station core was flooded with sunlight and its floor and terraces showed the beginnings of gardens and green space. Five levels of residential and work areas overlooked this space, alleviating the claustrophobia that struck so easily on base stations and long-distance transports. Two levels were still open as work crews completed the construction.

"As you will have seen during your approach here, the station is spindle-shaped with the gravity generator at the center which is now slightly below us." She gestured through the window. "The residential and administrative wings are operated at point eight of Bellac's gravity and dampened toward the station terminals." She turned to Boker. "The pointy ends."

Nova poked him again before he could retort with some wisecrack.

"As you noticed, gravity down at the elevator hub is much lighter, making work there more efficient and allowing for far larger containers. The same is true for the upper end of the station, where the solar collectors are almost weightless. Below that, of course are the two combat plane levels. A much grander landing bay is centrally located between the grow rings for the most spectacular view of the station upon approach. All civilians and off-duty personnel use those locks."

Nova left the interior wall to walk across the broad, empty concourse to look out over the exterior of the station. The central portion of the orbiter was surrounded by multi-level, mostly transparent rings where they would grow food and recycle water and gasses. Two of the rings were in place, a third was nearly complete. She saw people moving through them, partially afloat in the curving tubes. Against the black backdrop of space it looked as surreal as she remembered from past visits to places like these.

Some of the others also strolled over to where she stood with her hands pressed against the transparent wall.

"We maintain minimal gravity out there, basically just what the station pulls," the guide said. "The shells can be adjusted for radiation and light. The arms holding the rings are lined with conveyors that transport the bins of…"

Nova was no longer listening. "I'll see you later, Heiko," she whispered to Boker.

"Eh? Where are you going? I thought you wanted to see the place."

"Got something to do. They won't let us into the construction sites, anyway. Or the command center." She stepped away from the group and hurried upward along the curving concourse and then took a lift to the next level. The design of this station included improvements over those built before it but she knew her way around well enough. The exit she sought was a quarter of the way around the station from where she had left the tour.

"Evening," she greeted a technician standing near a workstation.

The Centauri looked up briefly and then back again when he realized that she was uniformed. "It's morning over there," he pointed through the transparent frontage at the planet. "Though my stomach says it's supper time. I'll never get used to it."

She smiled. "Me neither."

"Kind of out of your playpen, aren't you?" he said. "Don't often get pilots coming around up here."

"Grew up on a skyranch." She shrugged. "Lots of memories. And there's someone here I know. Maybe you can help me find him."

"Sure. Got a name?" The tech tapped on his screen to pull up a duty roster.

"Djari," she said and held her breath while he consulted his system. "Nathon Djari."

"Oh, I know that one. Human but from Bellac. You'll find him in the upper ring." He noticed her hesitation and gestured toward a service access ladder nearby. "Go on. Not restricted."

She followed his direction and climbed up into the transparent tunnel reaching out toward the farm rings. Humid air met her and she soon wished that she had left her jacket behind. Gradually, the pull of the station's gravity released her and she bounced lightly as she moved. Open service carts lined the wall to transport produce and supplies and probably some of the more adventurous staff to the ring. A transparent door swished aside when she approached and she was greeted by another draft of hot and humid air.

Some workers, more sensibly dressed than she was, looked up when she entered the ring but returned to their tasks when they saw her uniform. She declined an offer for a guided tour and was left to explore the space on her own.

So far, the growing platforms were empty except for a few racks of experiments. To Nova's untrained eye, the seedlings looked perky enough to eat, whatever they were. The transparent shell of the ring was fogged in places, hinting that some balancing and fine-tuning was still to be done here.

She bounced along the central pathway, respectfully dodging workers and their carts, prepared to pace the entire circumference of the ring to find Djari. Aisle upon aisle of trays marched off into the distance and she paused at scan each one. He would stand out among the garnet-skinned Bellacs working up here.

She had come about halfway, starting to get bored with this, when she finally spotted him near the end of one of the aisles. He stood turned away from her, busy with a tangle of tubes and gages. He wore the loose-fitting white coveralls made for this climate but she recognized his powerful build and the shock of sun-bleached hair even from this distance. It came as a bit of a surprise to her to feel a surge of excitement upon seeing him again.

"Djari!" she called out and jogged down the aisle.

He turned and a broad smile spread over his face when he saw her. The one that could light up the dark and that had kept her from utterly despairing during their brief captivity in Shon Gat. But as quickly as it appeared, it vanished and when she reached him he turned his face away from her.

Nova faltered. "Djari? No hug for your favorite officer?"

He glanced at her only briefly. "I… I hadn't expected to see you up here. They said you were at the gate now."

She frowned. "Yes, but we rotate often. What's wrong? Aren't you glad to see me?" She peered at him more closely. He did not resist when she reached out to turn his face toward her. "Gods, Djari," she breathed.

He faced her for a moment before turning away again. "Didn't turn out so pretty, did it?"

"Don't hide from me," she said. The laser blasts that had strafed his cheek and jaw had left a brutal wound on his face that was only now healing. "Why didn't you have that breezed," she said. "That's going to leave a scar." She looked down to see that his arm, below the rolled-up sleeve, was also a mass of twisted flesh.

"Too late now." He shrugged. "I don't need a pretty face up here."

"Can't you look at me when we're talking?"

"Can you?" He turned and she had to bite back a startled gasp. It wasn't the wound that troubled her; she had grown up among battle-scarred veterans and had seen worse than this. It was the look on his face that suddenly seemed so foreign. Something had erased the mild, open expression she had come to like and replaced it with anger and distrust.

"It's not so bad," she stammered, wondering if she sounded as lame to him as she did to herself. "Can they do anything for that?"

He shook his head. "No. After... after I left you at Shon Gat with your people I got caught up by a rebel group. They kept me for days, up in the hills. I don't know why. I was sick. And in pain. I finally got away and made my way back down and to the garrison." He bent to tuck his tools into a box by his feet. "By that time it was too late."

"We have an amazing exobiology clinic on Targon. There's a whole department specializing in Human—"

"Just leave it alone, Nova! I'm a civilian. How do you think I can get to Targon? Like you said, it's not so bad. It doesn't matter."

"Seems to matter to you or you'd look at me," she snapped back and regretted that immediately. "I'm sorry," she said more softly. "I'm so sorry about the whole thing. I wish they hadn't started to shoot. I wish you had stayed."

"I'd be dead now. Like the other civilians they murdered."

"They were... confused. It seemed like you were all armed."

His eyes narrowed. "There was no need for that and you know it, Lieutenant. That's what your people do if you give them the chance. And if you think that this was just some rare misfortune, you've been up in your plane for too long."

She reached out to touch him but he pulled away. "Please, Djari. I don't know what to say. How to make this right."

"You can't fix the world, Nova. This is what you've chosen. So live with it. You saw them down there! Maimed civilians, sick children, bodies in the streets. That's your war. Not Bellac's. Yours. You can't make it right any more than I can." He threw his hands up in a helpless gesture. "Why do you make excuses for this? Civilians get in the way. Your own people tried to break you. And you don't think there's something wrong with that?"

She frowned. "The Commonwealth was never meant to be a military force. It's about trade. Gods, Djari, if it weren't for groups like the Shri-Lan we'd need no military at all. We're spread out with few resources over just too much space. It can't possibly be perfect, no matter how hard we try." She looked around the endless rows of racks as if to find answers among the drip trays. "If… things happen so far out here, it's because of people, not some organization. People who don't care about rules. People who are in this for their own profit. And that includes Union members."

"More excuses," he grumbled, unconvinced. "I've seen enough. Neither of us belongs here."

"And yet, here you are," she said, gesturing at the farm flats with a sweep of her arm. "Working for the Union."

He said nothing for a moment. His eyes shifted to the orbiter seen through the transparent dome of the grow ring. "I'm working for Bellac," he said finally. He turned away. "You're working for Air Command."

She grasped his arm. "Don't do this, Djari," she pleaded, hurt by his dismissal of her and worried by the pain that obscured the gentle, nurturing man she had met in Shon Gat. "Please."

He turned back. For a moment she thought he would say something to show her that he was still in there somewhere.

115

He searched her face and raised a hand as if to touch her. Her breath caught when the angry tension shifted to something softer, perhaps something she recognized. Instead he snatched that hand away and covered it with the other as if to hide the scars on it. "Leave me alone," he said, his voice nearly a whisper. "Please just go away."

SEVEN

"So that's why I drink," Nova said and tipped back another thimble of what was not at all rotgut. Nor was this quiet, elegant lounge aboard the brand new orbiter even remotely comparable to the echoing rec halls that passed for bars around the ground bases. A skyranch was built for civilians and, given the isolation that comes with living in space, amenities were at the top of the health and wellness arrangements. It suited the pilots just fine.

Lieutenant Rolyn propped his face onto his palm and observed her critically. "Except that you don't."

"Don't what?"

"Drink. Much, anyway."

"I'm starting today," she said and tipped the jar over her glass for another shot.

"You'll puke," Heiko Boker, the other officer at the table, warned.

She shrugged. The two of them had lured her to the lounge at the end of today's shift, determined to cheer her up, or so they said. She suspected that they were mainly driven by curiosity.

The days since her painful encounter with Djari had

passed like sand through an hour glass. She did her work steadily and without enthusiasm, letting the time pass between shifts with morose walks along the station's exercise ring or by sleeping too much. She wanted to return to him, talk more about what had happened, perhaps even convince him to turn to the post-trauma team to help him get over his anger. Shon Gat had changed him, somehow, of that she was certain.

Boker and Rolyn were less convinced of that. They had dragged the story out of her over several shots of very smooth spirits, which actually made her feel a little better, and then set to analyzing the problem as if they had gathered for a debrief.

"You gotta deal, Whiteside," Boker said. "For all you know he's a right bastard all the time. You were stuck with him for just a couple of days. Maybe he was trying to impress you."

"And get himself some bag time with you," Rolyn added. "Let's not forget that."

She shook her head. "I can't believe that."

"You don't think he was?" He raised a hand and counted off on his fingers. "You're behind front lines. It's tense. You've come to count on him keeping his shit together when others aren't and you're a scrumptious example of femality. Now you're alone. Boom. Nothing takes the pressure off more than a good hard…" He checked himself. "…lovemaking."

Nova rolled her eyes although the sporadic attempts of her squad mates to curb their more colorful language were as amusing as they were condescending. "That's not all it was."

"I've seen him around," Boker said. "That's one nice looking pedestrian." He batted his eyelashes at the ceiling. "Shoulders out to here, dreamy streaky hair, a smile that'll melt Aram's core and, I have to admit, a shapely backside. Nice catch, Whiteside."

"That is not all it was!"

"No?" Rolyn said. "Now you're up here where it's safe.

Lots of other bedmates to be found. You're a pilot and he's crew. Civilian, like Heiko said. Those worlds don't even fit together."

She frowned. "Does it always have to come down to just that?"

"Yeah." Boker watched her take another shot. "Come clear with us, Whiteside. You're not bemoaning a lost love. You're pissed because he ditched you."

She scowled at him.

"Ah, I'm right," he grinned. "You're too tough for this shit, admit it. You don't get mad crushes on some pretty thing you barely know. I can name a few fine-looking slabs of officer-hood that'd take you home in an instant and you barely even look their way. It's not what you're here for, Lieutenant, and they know it. But then you fall for Farmboy? I don't buy it."

She pushed her glass around the table. Compelling or not, attractive or not, Boker was probably right about Djari. His rejection of her had stung. She hadn't encountered anything like it since a brief infatuation with a senior at the academy on Magra. "I just want to help him," she said. "He seems so lost."

"You're not helping anyone by letting this get to you," Rolyn said. "Let him sort out his own issues. You've got enough to deal with."

She looked up, sharply. "Like what?"

He smirked and elbowed Boker. "Do we tell her?"

His friend took a surreptitious look around the lounge as if about to reveal a secret of momentous impact. A few officers chatting over the drinks, couples having dinner, some civilians enjoying some sort of celebration. No one seemed interested in overhearing their conversation.

Nova gave his arm a playful punch. "Come on, Rolie. Now you got me curious."

"Don't tell the others. Lady Patrina is coming up. Inspection. Some engineers came in from Targon to go over the rings but she'll be here to give us a comb-through."

"The general?" Nova said. "How do you know?"

"We have our sources," Boker said disdainfully. "Make sure your shoes are polished. She's not been pleasant since the Shon Gat thing."

Nova sat back. "Please tell me we're doing a red flag for her!" A major military exercise like that counted fully toward the flying hours she needed for her next qualification.

They understood her excitement. "So it's told," Boker said. "And we'll get one day notice. The pilots, I mean." His expression grew a little more somber. "Dakad's going to need you to shine, Nova. He's going to put you on the Red team, I'm sure. Forget about your farmer. This is business."

She nodded. Red team meant that she would fly an enemy Shrill rather than her far more familiar Kite. A disadvantage in this mock battle but a position granted to only the more accomplished pilots. Another very solid highlight on her record. "I'll go crazy if he doesn't. When's this happening?"

"A few days. They're delivering the Shrills to the Old Man so we don't get wise to this. Already have a command center set up."

"Ah," she grinned. "You got this intel out of the crew. The techs have to be in on this." The moon called Old Man by Bellac's people had served as a base for microgravity exercises before. Setting a transport down on its surface was the easiest way to establish a livable environment for those monitoring the action. Still, placing the rally points and game beacons required more than just landing a ship.

"What? No. I seduced the Air Boss. Honest. She let it all spill in the throes of passion."

"Yah, right. Last time I saw you two together she asked you if you were better at cleaning latrines than landing your plane."

"It's all a front," he said. "She's mad about me."

Rolyn reached over and scrubbed Boker's closely-cropped head with his knuckles. "The boy is delusional."

Nova was not the only pilot thrilled that Boker and Rolyn's gossip turned out to be unusually accurate. Two days of rising excitement and endless speculation later, a cruiser from Bellac arrived, bringing with it General Patrina Ausan and a delegation of native governors and civilian engineers. Air Command's defensive measures up here on the orbiter were not the focus of their visit and, after an inspection of the pilots and soldiers in formal attendance, they were hustled into the grow rings to admire their future source of food and profits.

It was nearly time to turn in for the night when a last-minute assembly was called and the pilots gathered in the upper fighter craft hanger. Nova joined Boker, Rolyn and Lieutenants Nieri and Sulean to await the longed-for announcement. She gave a quick thumbs-up to her roommate Jianna, a member of Caga squad. Some of the technicians loitered near the back to watch.

The hall fell silent when Lieutenant Colonel Thedris, commander of Skyranch Twelve, and General Ausan, commander of all Air Command operations on Bellac, stepped onto a repair platform at the end of the hangar. The general made a brief speech that could probably apply to any military outfit doing its job on any of a dozen Union planets. But, finally, she announced the exercise and did not mind when the cheers from the pilots interrupted the presentation.

Each of the squadron leaders stepped forward to assign roles to their pilots. Seven Cagas and six Cet squad members were to fly defense, along with six of Nova's squad. Captain Dakad took his turn last. "I seem to have been elected to command the 'rebel' wing this time," he said, awkward with the informality of the moment. He glanced over his data sleeve.

Boker gripped Nova's elbow. When they were named to fly the quick, highly unstable enemy Shrills, both of them jumped up at once. More names were announced but she heard none of that.

"I'll never say anything mean about Dakad ever again," Boker said.

"You just hope those Shrills are glued together properly."

Rolyn sounded worried. "Those are captured enemy planes. Junk, in other words."

"Have some faith in our techs," Boker said. "And hope they remembered to take the fire out of those guns, 'cause I'm going to climb all over your six, brother!"

Nova pinched him to shut him up as Dakad gave instructions. "The Red team leaves after breakfast for the Old Man. The shuttle will be on Deck Two. Green team is taking the Kites directly. You'll get parking instructions upon arrival. Video coverage will be shown in the lounges. General Ausan will join us on the moon as well." He seemed to pick Boker out of the crowd. "So behave yourselves."

* * *

Nova was keyed up and ready to fly when she stepped through the door separating the pilots' quarters from the lower of the two combat flight decks long before any of them really needed to be there. As always, she felt the strange sense of displacement when she moved from the sound-baffled, muted corridors into the noisy, echoing clamor of the hangars. She walked down the long by-way, passing the closed chutes used by the Kites to the air locks designed for larger ships. Some of the other pilots were also already out here, impatient to head to the moon.

"Nova!"

She stopped to look around for the familiar voice. "Djari?" She waited while he hurried toward her. Oddly, it felt like she was seeing someone she had known for a long time. Had he really been on her mind that much? She smiled tentatively. "What are you doing up here?"

He held up a package, still out of breath. "New seeds just came in."

She groped for words, unsure of the moment and unprepared for this meeting. Ahead of her, Lieutenant Sool had turned to wait for her. She waved him onward.

Djari hesitated and the moment grew more awkward. "I hadn't expected to see you here, either," he said finally.

"What, on the flight deck? I work here."

He blinked. "I meant now. Don't you do the later shift?"

"Special exercise." She gestured to the transparent wall between the airlocks where the shuttle as well as General Ausan's cruiser stood ready for departure. "We're going to the moon."

"Can I talk to you?"

She looked to the ships again and then back at him, undecided.

"Please," he said. "I... I've been wanting to... apologize, I guess. Just give me a few minutes."

Nova peered into his face and something there seemed so miserable and urgent that she relented. The ships were not yet ready to leave, anyway. She followed Djari into one of the ready rooms overlooking the busy air lock area. "I'm not angry with you," she said to him. "You have reason for the way you feel."

He shook his head. "No. I was wrong to treat you like that. You're not like the others. I saw that on Shon Gat. I have no right to talk to you that way. Been losing sleep over it." He smiled crookedly. "So I talked to... to some people. I was wrong and I'm sorry. I wanted you to know that."

She smiled back at him. He did seem to be more his old self again, the way she had met him. She resisted the impulse to reach up to brush aside that rebellious shock of hair that seemed to constantly fall over his eyes. "You're not trained for... this. I'd be bitter, too, after what happened."

"I was afraid to call on you. Didn't think you'd ever talk to me again."

"I don't hold a grudge," she said. "Been kind of worried about you." She frowned when she looked past him through the open door and over the deck. Outside, the general's shuttle had moved away from the lock where it halted to await departure clearance. But it seemed strangely off-kilter, as if it were slowly rolling over; an unlikely maneuver while still within the station's gravity well. Someone ran toward the lock. Something flew past the window.

Nova lunged forward and threw herself at Djari to shove him backward and over a short podium step to the floor. A massive explosion roared through the open hangar space, muted only by the internal shielding. Its pressure wave was enough to shatter the window and collapse the doorframe of the ready room, showering them with shards and twisted pieces of metal. Nova pressed her face to Djari's chest until the noise had subsided. Alarms brayed into the brief silence that followed.

She came to her feet to look out into the devastated hangar. The locks that had just moments ago supported the two ships were gone. Massive, warped metal shapes littering the interior reminded of some familiar parts. Casualties, mostly hangar jockeys and a few troops, were scattered among the wreckage. Overhead lights had turned orange as soon as the shield generators had detected the change of pressure. Already, security personnel arrived to assess the situation. "Gods, the shuttle!" she gasped, frantically trying to remember which of her wing mates had already boarded. Sool, maybe also Drayson and Xiachiu. She hoped Boker was running late as usual.

"Djari?" she turned back to him. He was still on the floor and still clutching his package of seeds. There was blood on it. "Djari!"

He groaned. A piece of the window transparency had cut deep into his shoulder. "I think I hit my head."

"Lie still. I'll get help."

"I'll be all right. You?"

"Not even a scratch." She hurried outside to flag down a medic before returning to his side.

"You know, maybe we shouldn't keep meeting like this," he said through clenched teeth as he sat up. Blood poured from his wound and he twisted to get a look at it. "Do you ever have a quiet day or something?"

"All pilots to scramble," they heard the Air Boss snap over the com unit at her wrist. "Roof deck is a go."

"They didn't get all of the decks," she translated as she

tapped her com unit. "Whiteside able."

"They? You think that was an attack?"

"We always think that." She stood aside when someone arrived with a med kit. "Shuttles don't just blow up. We'll talk later."

She raced to a companionway at the end of the platform, dodging damaged equipment and harried personnel along the way. Two other pilots followed her to the upper deck, also not bothering to wait for the lift which might not even be operational. She stopped near the supply shed to pick up a helmet. It did not fit as well as her own, already waiting for her in the Shrill she was to have used today, but the interface matched and that was all that mattered.

"Rally at Launch Three," Dakad's voice came from her com sleeve.

She changed direction and ran along a row of Kites to where he waited for his squad. Ground crew paced up and down, scanning for explosives. "Rolie!" she cried out with relief when she saw the young Lieutenant. His constant companion, Heiko Boker, was not in sight. She did not dare to ask.

Dakad also wasted no time with roll call to find out what was left of his squadron. The next explosion could well happen on this level. "Let's get these planes in the air," he snapped. "Section One: Whiteside lead for tether." His eyes found Rolyn and moved on to another pilot to assign her wingman and then the rest of the unit. "I'll lead the array defense. Rolie, you're with me."

They scrambled to their assigned Kites and, one by one, entered the chutes to launch into space.

From here protocol took over. Nova led her flight around the station and down to the tether where they took up defensive positions around the bottom of the ranch, its most vulnerable part. The cargo pods had stopped and each level had been sealed off from the next. She sent two Kites down to the halfway point.

"Nothing on sensors," Sulean muttered needlessly. They

all saw that. While an enemy fighter could conceivably slip past their eyes and make it to the station, nothing with the power they had witnessed would easily approach the skyranch without notice.

"Tower concurs," Dakad said from his position above the solar arrays. "We'll stay out until all decks are cleared."

"What do you think—"

"I want no chatter, no speculation, no talk at all. Continue patrol pattern until all clear."

They fell silent, sweeping the area with sensors and eyes, swinging wide when a swarm of service shuttles issued from the lower decks. The blast had been powerful enough for some pieces to escape the orbiter's gravity and a scatter of debris slowly spread out from the site of the detonation. Suited-up ground crew searched the exterior for bodies and evidence. The pilots felt useless out here, doing little more than minding their expensive planes without an enemy in their sights.

How many had they lost? Nova thought about Sool, a quiet and polite Caspian who seemed to forever stumble over his outsized feet. He had three mates, as far as she knew, but no children yet. Where was Boker? Floating around out here in small pieces? Still on the station, now perhaps in the medical center? Or maybe in the small morgue where bodies were kept until someone claimed them. She thought about Rolie, now under Dakad's watchful eye, no doubt beside himself with worry about his friend.

And what about Djari? He had fought whatever demons had followed him from Shon Gat to reach out to her only to be quite literally knocked back down by the Union's never-ending conflicts. She watched a med-evac plane speed away from the station; casualties too badly wounded to be treated up here. Djari's injuries had not been severe but she worried, anyway.

Hours passed before two cruisers arrived from the planet, no doubt investigators from the base at Siolet. They hovered briefly and then slipped into the upper landing bays.

Dakad's voice rasped into her earpiece. "All clear. Section One, return to base. Proceed to ready room and wait for Section Two."

They obeyed silently, relinquished their Kites and then took their seats in the pilots' lounge. Nova had peeled out her flight suit down to her tights and body shirt and huddled in her chair with her legs drawn tight to her body. There was nothing to say. Nothing to do but wait.

Dakad arrived with his section and another officer. He was still checking communications on his data sleeve. Everyone's eyes were on the door to see which of their comrades were going to join them. Nova shifted over to sit with Lieutenant Rolyn.

"Men," Dakad said with an apologetic nod to Nova. "We have some info but they'll be sifting the hangar for a while. Initial reports point to the general's cruiser as the target. I regret to inform you that General Ausan and most of her crew were lost. No explosives found so far but they have not ruled out sabotage. The shuttle got in the way of the blast. We've got eleven ground crew injured, two dead. Among the pilots, in the vicinity were Tashti, Khateka and Whiteside. Tashti is down in the med station." He tugged on his nose before continuing. "All hands aboard the shuttle were lost to explosive decompression due to a rupture of the starboard side of the ship. Shuttle pilot Anina, three Caga squad pilots." He glanced at Rolyn. "The other four were ours: Drayson, Ash Ngava, Sool, and Boker. Their bodies have been recovered."

Dakad droned on about damage to the station, which was confined to the hangar and central platform, expectations of replacements for the lost pilots, adjusted schedules. Nova had grasped Rolyn's hand in both of hers but whether that was for her comfort or his was a moot point.

She had lost fellow pilots in battle and some of them had been friends. She remembered Chidi Lux, her roommate on her first assignment and a decidedly free spirit, taken down by an enemy fighter over Tannaday. There had been a training accident on Magra that had cost two cadets. She had been in a few major engagements with heavy casualties on both sides. But never this many of what Dakad had called 'ours', all at once. Never people with whom she had just finished breakfast. Never this pointlessly. And why Boker? she thought and then looked over the somber, disheartened faces of her squad mates. And why Reko?

Apparently Dakad had finished. Nova looked up when Sulean bent over her seat. "You guys all right?" he said.

Rolyn frowned as if his words were in another language. At length he shrugged. Then nodded. Someone came to take him away, possibly to get very drunk.

"You coming, too, Nova?" Sulean asked.

She blinked. "Huh? Oh. I'm going down to the hospital." She hurried from the flight deck and down to the support level of the station. The clinic there was very new; today's victims were the first casualties of anything more worrisome than construction crew injuries and stomach upsets. She stopped a service staff member to ask about Djari.

"He's been released," she was told rather curtly.

"Can you tell me where I can find him?"

The clerk consulted his data pad with an air of great impatience. Nova looked around. The hospital level was designed to service a full complement of five hundred souls once the station was fully operational. Surely today's half dozen casualties did not tax their systems. She bit back a reprimand, unsure of how one even dealt with civilians here.

"He is quartered on Level Two, cabin Six."

"How is Lieutenant Tashti?"

The clerk's eyes swept over Nova to find the insignia band around her bare upper arm, perhaps wondering how much authority that carried with it. Finally, he called up the pilot's profile. "She is sleeping. Come back later."

Nova left the hospital and made her way back up to the second residential level. She found Djari's room and knocked urgently, not even sure why she needed to see him so badly.

"Nova!" he exclaimed when he saw her. He wore only a short kilt favored by Bellac natives and a thin plaster over his injured shoulder.

She rushed into his room and when she reached for him he could do little more in his surprise than hold her close. She felt his strong arms wrap around her and buried her face in the curve of his neck, just wanting to stay there for a long time. It felt like it had in Shon Gat and she let his presence soothe her as it had before.

"Are you all right?" he said softly. His hands stroked her back.

She shook her head still pressed against his skin. "No, I'm not. Seven of them gone. My friends. And half the damn ground crew. General Ausan! All dead."

"I'm so sorry," he said.

She finally lifted her face. "I'd be gone, too, if it weren't for you. I was supposed to be on that ship."

He brushed a few loose strands of hair from her cheek. "And you probably saved my neck with that tackle."

"We keep thinking this can't happen to us, but it does. I feel so bad. I wish there were something I could do."

He wrapped his arms around her again. "So do I. I wish I could make this all go away for you."

She looked up into his eyes. "You can."

"Nova," he began, trying to look away and failing. His eyes shifted to her lips. She felt his chest expand with a hitching breath. "This isn't right," he whispered.

"It is."

Djari shook his head, the gesture slow and unfinished. He gripped her arms as if to pull them away but then he did not. "You're upset," he said thickly. "Just cry."

She pressed more tightly against his bare chest. "I don't need to cry. I need you. Make it better."

Some unclear, wordless sound escaped him before he bent to kiss her. It was not a gentle kiss nor was she looking for that. His hands and lips were demanding and perhaps he needed her just as much as she craved his touch. They staggered on their feet and he pushed her against the wall. When he gripped her thighs to lift her up she felt his growing excitement not just by his hungry kiss but through the thin fabric that separated their bodies.

She froze when a cold stab of fear intruded upon the moment.

He eased back as if sensing the shift and turned to carry her to his cot. She looked up at him as he placed her there, moving more gently as he joined her in carefully removing her clothes. Their hands and lips continued their exploration and it did not take long before she reached for him, assured once more that nothing he did could ever hurt her. She received him joyfully, moving with him in a rising fervor of passion that, once peaked in a blinding burst of ecstasy, left them gasping for air and utterly spent.

He shifted her to sprawl across his chest, making the most of his narrow bed. "You know," he said when he was able to speak again. "I think now I know why they call you Nova."

She looked up. "Hey, my daddy named me that!"

"It was a good choice." His thumb stroked across her cheek for a thoughtful moment. "Your smile is back, Sunshine."

She lowered her head again and sighed deeply. "Because of you."

"I've thought about you since… since Shon Gat. You've been on my mind. I've never known someone like you. But you're so far away."

"I'm right here," she said, quite aware of what he meant. "And not going anywhere soon. Well, unless your roommate decides to come home."

"Don't have one. The crew is so small right now. We're still experimenting and balancing the systems. The workers won't arrive for a while yet."

"Is that why you have room for all this stuff here?" She pointed at stacks of flat, unlabeled boxes piled on the other bed in the room. A collection of analysis tools cluttered a narrow shelf along with small bottles of colored substances. "Bringing your work home with you?"

"I guess," he said. "Some pilfering going on in the rings. I kept losing trays of our nutrient experiments, so I just packed them up. The stuff is expensive."

"Hey, maybe by the time the rest of the crew gets here you'll have your own suite. Something tells me you're not just a worker."

"Why do you say that?"

"You don't strike me as someone who's happy counting seedlings."

"True. I'd like to continue work on hybridizing some of Bellac's produce. Longer daylight hours can make all the difference. Lots of good ideas coming from the other ranches."

She brushed her lips over his smooth chest. "Well, as long as you get your own room. It's hard to sneak into the pilot quarters if you don't belong there."

A small, vertical line appeared between his brows. "Is that what you have in mind? A secret lover among the ground pounders?"

She pursed her lips. "Well, yes."

"So it's: I like you, you like me, let's sleep together?"

She shifted her eyes away from his watchful scrutiny and leaned over the edge of the bed to fish for her discarded shirt. "Should there be more?"

He watched her pull her shirt over her head and then attempt to untangle her tousled hair. "You don't have to run from me, Nova. This is not a day for promises. Take what you want; I won't ask for anything more."

"I know," she said softly. "You make me feel safe here." Then she grinned mischievously. "Of course, we might fall madly in love and then I'd have to become a farmer or you join the ranks of neglected pilot spouses."

"They're neglected?"

"Yeah, you don't get to take one with you until you rank higher. It's expensive."

"Doesn't sound like much fun." He pushed her shirt out of the way again and then pulled her down to nuzzle her tenderly.

"I should go," she said and closed her eyes.

"Yes," he agreed. "In a while."

EIGHT

Her quarters were empty when she returned there. Her roommate, a somewhat bland and overly organized Centauri pilot, had left word that members of all three squads of their wing were gathered in one of the lounges.

Nova felt a twinge of guilt, mostly because the memory of Djari's skillful hands on her body still lingered in her memory. She dropped her clothes to the floor and stepped into the tiny decon chamber, letting it rinse away the pain and the pleasure that this day had brought. The thought of joining her dispirited team mates filled her with dread but she worried about Rolyn. Drayson was as well-liked as Boker and no doubt the casualties who belonged to the other squad had left a hole in their friends' lives as well.

She wished Djari was here to join them. His gift for putting others at ease would be welcomed. But even as the thought passed through her musings, she realized that it would not be so. The distance between civilians and Air Command pilots was more than rank. She had been right to quip about falling in love and he had responded in kind. They were worlds apart in the distance her next assignment may bring, in ambition, and in temperament.

Nova dried her hair and caught it up in a loose knot before slipping into a sleeveless blouse and knee-length tights to join her squad. She didn't want to feel like a soldier tonight. She had missed dinner while in Djari's much more sustaining embrace but she doubted the others had eaten, either.

When she arrived in the lounge she found them all as depressed as she had expected them to be. Talk around the tables was subdued; the staff kept the music somber and muted, drinks were dispensed in large quantities. Nova slid into a bench where Rolyn stared into his glass while some of her squad mates sat in awkward silence.

She gave his shoulders a quick squeeze.

"You checked out all right?" he said, barely looking up.

"Huh?"

"At the hospital."

"Yes, I didn't get hit. I went to check on the others. Tashti was sedated."

"I saw her earlier," Lieutenant Cierol said. "She's got internal damage and a broken leg. They transferred her to Siolet."

"Do we know what happened?" Nova looked up to signal for a drink.

"They're still combing through things," Sulean, across from her, said. "It's pretty clear that the general was the target. We're lucky that Thedris was still topside."

"Their timing was damn excellent," Nova said.

He nodded. "Whoever planned this must have known that there'd be pilots on that shuttle. Worthwhile target, besides making Deck Two totally useless for a while."

"Could be a warning of more to come," she said. "Did Shri-Lan claim this business?"

"No idea. I'd expect so."

"I wish someone would just wipe that whole bloody faction out," Rolyn exclaimed forcefully. There were dark rings under his bloodshot eyes. "We know where they are half the time. Let's just finish this already!"

Nova moved to cover his hand with hers but he pulled it away. "We wait till they hit us and then we slap them around a bit. That's it. Where's the offense? The pre-emptive?"

"We do hit them, Rolie," Nova said. "You were there when we took that Rhuwac nest out. And the transport going to Siolet before that."

"Those fucking Rhuwacs are nothing! I'm talking about taking out the damn rebel hideouts. They're not even rebels! Rebels have at least some goddamn ideology, like the Arawaj faction does. The Shri-Lan are nothing but thieves and smugglers. Let's just get this over with."

"They're tucked in with the locals," Nora reminded him.

"So what! If someone's hiding rebels let them pay for that. We've got twenty-something fighters hanging around up here doing nothing. Fifty on the ground just around the Rim. What are we waiting for?"

"You don't mean that, Rolie," Nova said. She had seen the damage rebel presence did even when Air Command was not bent on scorching the lot. Had he?

He looked around the circle of worried faces. "No," he said glumly. "I guess I don't."

"We'll be concentrating on the jumpsite once we own it," Sulean reminded him. "We can choke them off at the front door. It'll make a big difference here."

Nova listened to talk of attacks and rebels and sabotage until she felt like she might slide from her bench in a puddle of despair. Unable to take much more, she finally excused herself and left the wake, not with another stab of guilt when she felt immediately better after the door to the lounge slid shut behind her.

Not ready for sleep, she wandered through the corridors, finally stopping at the observation window overlooking the open core of the orbiter. She watched a couple stroll through the half-finished green space below her and thought about Djari, of his perfect smile, his soft words and his hands on her body. She wished for him now, here with her. When she let her eyes wander pensively to the stars outside the dome she saw the terrace of the administrative level still brightly lit.

What was going on behind those closed doors? The investigators would be busy going over video recordings, dispersal patterns, injuries, communications and hundreds of other details that were part of the sabotage. None of this would be shared with the pilots and, not for the first time, she wished she were part of that larger view of their military. Those who really understood the rebel factions and who planned for their elimination fascinated her. Like her fellow pilots, she was merely a weapon pointed at a certain target at a certain time. Working diligently toward gaining rank and distinctions would perhaps someday bring her up to that level below the skylight. Until then, she could only wonder about what truly drove their mighty Union.

She continued around the promenade and climbed up to the flight levels. Access to the lower tier of air locks was cordoned off and she stood at the barrier to watch workers in color-coded coveralls still comb through the site while others were already working on repairs. Structural engineers were busy with lasers and analyzers to determine the damage to the adjacent fighter chutes and hangars. Someone was arguing somewhere. Someone else was laughing. As out of place as that seemed, it comforted her.

"Almost bought the farm, didn't you?" a low voice rolled out to her left.

She turned to peer into the shadows. A hulking figure leaned against the wall, one foot raised and propped up against it. She gasped and took a step back. "Beryl."

"In the flesh," he replied but his eyes traveled down along her body when he said the last word, giving it more meaning than it needed. Nova suppressed a shudder and took another step backward.

"No need to run away," he said with a lazy wave of his hand. "Not scared, are you?"

"Disgusted, maybe," she said, aware of the sudden pounding of her heart, unwilling to show the fear that gripped her even here, well in sight of the ground crew and under the scrutiny of the overhead security cameras. She wished for her gun, just to feel its comforting weight at her side. But, unlike on the ground bases, pilots did not walk around an orbiter fully armed.

He snorted something like laughter. Nova frowned and narrowed her eyes to study his shadowed face. His eyes glittered in the dark and his voice had a hollow, dragging tone. The body slumped against the wall was anything but battle-ready.

"You're stoned!" she gasped. The symptoms he showed looked like the result of ingesting a few pinches of *mince*. Likely, given his size, more than a few pinches.

His sneer faded from his lips. Slowly, he pushed away from the wall and towered above her until she had to tip her head back to look up at him. She refused to back off another step.

"You haven't learned to mind your own business yet, Lieutenant," he said. "Others have, and they're still healthy."

"Don't you threaten me," she said in a relatively firm voice.

He looked over her shoulder when another member of the security team strolled into the hangar entrance from the hall. "Or what?" Beryl said. "You think it's worth reporting me? Again?"

She glanced over to the other Centauri silently smirking at her. Was it worth it? A drug-addled soldier who already bore her a grudge? Whose equally ruthless squad would walk through fire if he told them to?

"Get out of my way," she snarled and stalked away without looking at either one of them again.

* * *

The days that followed aboard Skyranch Twelve were both a trial and a joy for Nova. The mood among the pilots had not lifted. The station was on alert but the patrols they flew were merely exercises and make-work and did little to keep their minds from wandering. Every one of them ached to get down to the planet surface where the chance of striking back at the rebel was far more likely.

The leadership recognized their unrest and there was talk about a rotation back to Rim Station to let them all blow off some steam in active patrols.

Nova was torn about that. Nothing gave her more joy than sitting at the controls of her fighter plane, feeling it respond to her mental touch, watching her shadow race over the planet surface. She longed for a deep space assignment but flying within an atmosphere such as Bellac's made the heart race.

But so did Djari. Nova did not see him on the day after their first intimate encounter, almost glad as she still brooded over both the loss of her wing mate and her ugly encounter with Beryl. It would not do for her to fling herself into Djari's arms every time she needed comforting like a little girl. She was stronger than that, she thought. Maybe not strong enough to march up to the station commander and give him her view of Beryl and his men. That seemed more like suicide.

She came to him again the following day and the one after that. He welcomed her into his quiet, safe place where they made love and talked a while about nothing at all and then perhaps made love again before parting ways. She reveled in his attention and nearly craved the powerful body that lifted her own to such heights. A rotation to the planet was little enticement to leave his bed.

"Djari?" Nova said when, at the end of a far too long and uneventful shift, her soft knock on his door brought no response. She checked the time to assure herself that he would be expecting her now, at the end of his own day. He had given her access to some of his files and when she checked his location she was told that he was in his cabin. She knocked again and still there was no response.

She placed her hand over the access panel beside the door and, once recognized, stepped into his room. It was a bit of a tumble and Nova wondered if she could dare tidy up in here.

Even after just a few days together, his laid-back ways had made it easy to feel unreservedly comfortable around him.

Deciding against housekeeping chores, she pondered over some slides scattered beside an analyzer on the small desk. Curious, she peered into the apparatus to see cell structures which told her absolutely nothing. Djari probably felt the same about her navigational charts. She frowned when she noticed his com band among the equipment, left behind here and the reason why the station's system thought him to be in his room.

No cause for alarm, she told herself. Djari gladly worked long hours to ensure the success of this new ranch but the thought of being so easily summoned by his superiors for their never-ending emergencies and special projects irked him. She had seen him without the unit before. Likely, she thought, he was on his way here, perhaps with a bottle of wine cadged from the lounge as he had done before.

But she tired of waiting and decided to make her way to the upper grow ring to look for him there. Security had tightened since she had last come this way. She submitted to a retina scan which, once her credentials were verified, exempted her from having her pockets checked and motives questioned.

She asked a few of the workers and biologists about Djari before she was directed to his supervisor, busy at a small work station overlooking the long curve of the ring. He was deeply immersed in whatever he was viewing on his screens and apparently oblivious to the breathtaking view of the planet through the transparent ceiling. She looked up at it for a while, feeling a little vertigo and a lot of awe. The station itself did not spin and the gray, cloud-swathed planet hovered motionless in the distance.

It was a while before he noticed her standing there. "Yes..." he squinted at her armband. His black hair was far longer than what was currently fashionable among Centauri and was caught up in a disorderly knot atop his head. "Officer Whiteside?"

"I'm sorry to interrupt. I'm looking for Nathon Djari."

"He's off duty."

"I know that. I thought perhaps he was working late."

The botanist shook his head. "A man's got to rest," he said and, with another look at her, added, "or whatnot. More to life than work, you know." He returned his attention to his screens.

"Do you know where he might be?" she said, amused.

"I think he said something about taking the shuttle down to the surface. Or maybe that was yesterday."

"He was here yesterday."

"Well, then it was today."

"Did he say why?" Nova asked, puzzled.

"A man's time is his own," the Centauri said philosophically. "I don't ask."

"Of course. Thank you." Nova left him to his work and returned to the station, pondering. Civilians were not often given the privilege of taking trips to the surface unless whatever shuttles traveled there had the room to spare. Why would Djari not have mentioned a trip to Bellac? They had spent so much time together these past few days, surely something like this would have come up.

She strolled to the pilots' favored lounge and found Rolyn staring into his glass of ale. He had kept to himself these past few days, at a loss without Boker who had been his constant source of entertainment and vexation. They chatted quietly for a while, avoiding talk of the dead pilot in favor of less painful subjects. Eventually, she coaxed him into joining her for some dinner instead of another glass of the limpid, nearly flavorless beer and then turned him over to Nieri and two Caga squad pilots who preferred games of chance over alcohol.

Rolyn was an excellent pilot and she worried about him. Although Dakad had eased up on all of them since the explosion on the flight deck he would not put up with poor performance because of hangovers.

The day's shuttle from Bellac was due to dock at the main

gate and Nova took the lift there, eager for a few moments with Djari before needing to turn in. Some of their recent evenings together had stretched far into the night and the lack of sleep was beginning to affect her in the cockpit. Then again, she thought, he might have decided to spend the night on the surface and she'd be getting all the sleep she needed tonight.

The passenger bay was already bustling with arrivals when she stepped out of the lift. She scanned over guards on a shift rotation, a visiting Caspian family with a gaggle of children, grow ring workers, a few officers back from shore leave.

Then she saw Djari leap down the ramp to get ahead of a wheeled bin. He was casually dressed in a white shirt that contrasted nicely with his deeply tanned skin and her breath caught a little when he beamed a broad smile at one of the crew. He chatted briefly with the woman rolling the bin from the shuttle and then walked to the main corridor before Nova could call out to him.

She hurried after him, hoping to catch him before he got to the lifts. But he continued past them into the main concourse, perhaps on his way to find a late dinner. The Green House Eatery there was developing a terrific selection of Bellac delicacies far beyond the usual list of interspecies mainstays offered by the mess hall. She was about to call his name when he stopped abruptly. A uniformed guard strode toward him. Nova groaned when she recognized Captain Beryl.

She hung back, curious, while the two men spoke. Djari's back was turned to her and she saw little of their exchange. The expression on Beryl's face was as unpleasant as always. There came a moment when he raised his hand and Djari took a quick step back as if surprised by the gesture. A moment later Beryl looked over Djari's shoulder to see her walking toward them. He sneered and left the corridor.

Djari turned. "Nova! How did you know I'd explode if I didn't get to see you tonight?"

She stepped into his embrace and kissed him quickly. "I looked for you earlier. They told me you'd gone down."

He nodded. "Yes, I got volunteered to pick up the swampers. Too fragile to ship up with the elevator. Very tasty, though. They'll grow like mad up here."

"You didn't take your com unit?"

A trace of a frown appeared on his face. "We get the cheap toys. That unit is only good for up here. So I don't bother."

"Oh. Right." She looked into the direction that Beryl had taken. The concourse was now deserted except for a few construction workers ambling to their dinners and showers. "What did Beryl want?"

"Just talking. Why do you have more questions than kisses for me, Sunshine?"

She shrugged. "I don't like that man."

This time his frown was more pronounced. "Have you had dealings with him?"

"Not good ones." She did not look at him. "He's... not a good soldier. That's all. His ways are... undisciplined. It's not the way we're meant to be."

"Well, as I've been telling you, Lieutenant." Djari softened this reminder with a gentle smile. "What you're meant to be and what some of you are... Well, they're not the same. I guess it gets the job done. Beryl seems... efficient."

"Was he rude to you?" she asked carefully. For all his openness and what she hoped was trust for her, Djari would not easily admit to having fallen victim to Beryl and his gang. Their petty tortures would only confirm his view of Air Command's methods.

"No." He took her hand. "I have an idea. Come, I want to show you something. Down by the hub."

Puzzled, she followed him to the lifts leading to the lower tiers of the station. He would say nothing more until they reached the public corridor outside the elevator shipping level. He nudged her to walk ahead of him to the end. "In there," he pointed to an unmarked door. "It's unlocked."

"You're so mysterious today," she said, utterly curious now. What could there possibly be to see at the docks? A new ship, perhaps? Some remarkable delivery?

They slipped through the door to enter a shaft containing only a set of rungs embedded in the wall. It looked much like a small cargo lift on which someone had forgotten to actually install the car. Looking down, she saw a metal floor with lines painted on it. Someone walked down there and she realized that she was looking into the access area to the elevator. Djari pointed upward. She climbed the ladder ahead of him and stepped out onto a catwalk of sorts at the top.

"What is this?"

"I don't know, but it's really beautiful."

"It is?" The walkway up here formed a ring around the top of the shipping area, circling the tether, she assumed. The construction was not finished here and they passed piles of building materials, coils of wire and conduit, debris and tools.

He halted for a moment to peer around a gap in the wall and then gestured to her to scurry around him before they could be spotted by the workers below. "This is just a standard part of the orbiter design," he whispered. "Not likely to ever be used unless they get a lot of demand for sight-seeing up here. This gap here was meant for a staircase."

"Sight-seeing what?"

He ushered her into an enclosed space beside the gap in the wall and closed the door behind them. "Look," he said.

They had come to a curved room whose ceiling and most of one wall was made of a slightly domed, transparent window. Nova gripped his arm when she looked up to see Bellac Tau above them like an enormous moon in the sky. She made out its continents and oceans, partially obscured by swirling cloud patterns. The tether itself extended from here and disappeared to a point on its way to the planet. The sun's light reflected by Bellac, along with the stars in the sky, was all that was needed to illuminate this space tonight. Standing close to the window, she felt as if she were floating in space. "Beautiful," she whispered.

"Isn't it lovely? We're actually at almost the lowest point of the orbiter and, technically, upside down. Come sit." He drew her to where someone had placed a thickness of foam padding.

She grinned. "You come here often? How did you find this place?"

"Poking around. I'm down here quite a bit when things come up from the base. Someone mentioned that there was an observation platform up here. If you look out long enough you feel like you're flying out there."

"What are those?" Nova pointed at a row of blue metal bins stacked in a corner.

"No idea." He sat on the pallet and pulled her down to lie beside him. "Look outside. This might not be such a big deal for you, Pilot Lady, but for me this is the next best thing to being out there."

"No, this is stunning." She laid down on her back and gazed up at the canopy of stars. They shimmered slightly behind the orbiter's shields as if seen through a planet's atmosphere rather than as the stark pinpricks of light she saw from her cockpit.

"I used to watch the stars from Bellac," he said and stretched out on his side, close to her. "On those rare nights when the skies are clear. And dream of traveling."

"To where?"

"Doesn't matter. Anywhere that's new. You must have seen many places."

"I've seen many Air Command bases. They all look the same. Although my parents made sure we took trips off-base as often as possible. I've been on a few of Magra's continents. Callas once. A trip to Phi Four a long time ago. I barely remember it. I want to travel to other places, too. Feyd sounds interesting. And I've heard a lot about Delphi."

"Feyd is dangerous to Humans and Delphi doesn't allow foreigners."

"And you think that'll stop me?" She raised her arms as if to embrace the night sky. "I am going to see them all. You just watch."

He leaned forward to kiss her softly. "You will, I'm sure."

"Yeah. Meanwhile, we have this." She tilted her head to let his lips travel over the skin of her neck. "And this is a very, *very* nice place to hide out." Vistas like the one before them existed in other parts of the station, but none so private and none where being seen with a member of the crew in such an intimate display would not raise questions.

He seemed to guess her thoughts and began to unfasten her shirt.

"What do you have in mind, sir?"

"Shh," he whispered. She shivered when he bared her to the sky and each other and his hand, calloused but infinitely gentle, moved over her body. "Wanted to see you like this, in the star light," he said. "A Nova among the stars."

She purred under his touch. "You are a poet. I told you." She gasped when he pulled on the string of her loose trousers. "Not here!" she whispered.

"I locked the door." He smiled when she did not resist losing the rest of her clothes and happily submitted to his questing fingers. She looked out into the endless expanse of time, thinking of nothing until she was swept away to somewhere out there, arching her back with a guttural groan that he silenced with his kiss. Still befuddled by the moment, she turned to him and he lifted her over his lap to watch her move languidly above him, outlined by the stars and a halo of hair. He held her for a long while after finding his own release in deep, shuddering waves of pleasure.

NINE

"Whiteside!"

Nova looked up from her breakfast bowl when the call cut through the chatter, the scrape of chairs on the bare floor, the clatter of dishes being stacked and sorted in the nearby kitchen. Lieutenant Sulean and her Caga squad roommate also scanned the mess hall to find Captain Dakad striding toward them. Nova slapped the com screen on her sleeve as if that would make it work properly. "I could have sworn I wound this thing up this morning."

Sulean snickered and nudged one of the replacement pilots who had finally arrived just two days ago. "He likes to shout. The com bands aren't conducive to shouting."

"He'd find a way," Nova mumbled. The day had barely begun and already Dakad had found some reason to bark.

"He scares me," the pilot said, not frightened enough to let it interrupt his breakfast.

Nova cast a curious glance his way. That Lieutenant Ko hailed from Feyd was clear by the deep brown of his skin, embellished on all exposed parts with intricate tattoos that carried much meaning for his people. Having seen him at his exercises, she knew that the patterns were not restricted to just his face and neck. But his long-limbed body was typically Centauri as was the black hair. Centauri and Feydans carried nearly identical DNA and most other Prime species were also not that far removed. This was as much a reason to suspect divine intention as much as some shared origin in another part of the galaxy, depending on one's viewpoint. Nova had no precise viewpoint but she found the possibility endlessly fascinating. Interspecies breeding was rare and often problematic and so generally not encouraged by those who had any say in the matter. Still, people had a way of getting together. Proof of that was sitting right here, slurping the last of his fruit soup.

The captain arrived at their table. "Saddle up, Whiteside. You're taking a few pedestrians back down to the Shon Gat garrison and then you'll pick up three more pilots while you're there. A bunch of day trippers want to go, too."

"Aye, sir." They still hadn't replaced the lost shuttle pilot and so the combat pilots had filled in for her, not averse to the break in routine or the chance to spend the occasional evening on the Siolet base.

"No layover. You're back here tonight."

"Thank you, sir," she said.

Dakad's narrowed eyes exuded disapproval while he tried to decide if sarcasm was involved in her reply. Seeing nothing on her guileless face, he spun and left them to their tea.

"Some day, Nova…" Sulean warned.

Her roommate smirked, like Lieutenant Rolyn well aware of how Nova was spending her downtime. "Something tells me she meant it."

Nova stood up. "Bus is leaving soon. Better be on it."

She left the mess and bypassed the restricted lifts leading to the fighter plane levels to take the one to the passenger concourse. The supply clerk supplied her with the latest gossip while issuing her the uniform used by non-military pilots. He also promised her a fresh flight suit upon her return, for which she was grateful. The suits had a way of picking up an unpleasant rankness well before new ones were issued.

She waited at the shuttle gate while security checked it once more for possible sabotage and then completed her own pre-flight inspection before allowing the passengers aboard. The civilians returning to the base were the last of the team still investigating the explosion on the flight deck. Despite Nova's carefully padded inquiries during the trip to the surface, none of them seemed inclined to discuss the case. She wondered if the supply clerk would have better luck with them. Perhaps he gave lessons in prying gossip out of people.

She landed them on the dusty airfield that served the elevator base garrison and saw them safely transferred to another plane leaving for Siolet. Then there was not much to do but wait for her new passengers. She knew no one here that she cared to visit. Her temporary squad during her stint as ground pounder was now manning Rim Station, her old base. She cared little for the ones here now, consisting mostly of troops either belonging to or afraid of Captain Beryl. She ambled to the garrison administrative building, craning her neck up at the elevator looming over the landscape. It was impossible to ignore.

It was cooler inside and she flapped the front of her uniform blouse to circulate the air under there while she filed her report with a bored clerk. "So where is everybody? I'm expected back topside today."

"Not here yet. Sandstorm grounded their skimmer. I'll tag you when they're ready to leave."

"Storm heading this way?" Although Shon Gat was officially cleared of militants now, the absolute least entertaining thing she could think of was to be grounded here overnight. Perhaps there was time to head to Camomas or one of the other towns instead.

"Nah. Blowing itself out over the flats. You'll be okay."

Nova looked out of a sand-encrusted window over the training grounds. A few grunts were jogging around out there, no doubt cursing the grit drifting into their lungs. How fortunate her own team was to be stationed aboard the skyranch with its new, clean exercise equipment and a view of the green space while doing their laps.

"Is the pilot here yet?" she heard a gruff voice through an open door.

"Yessir, right here," the clerk replied.

"Send him in."

Nova raised an eyebrow and walked into the commander's office where she saluted with the least amount of decorum she could get away with. "Major Trakkas," she said.

He looked up. "What are you doing down here, Whiteside?"

"Driving the bus."

"You air jockeys don't have enough to do," he muttered. He gave her a card. "Get over to the climber hub and pick up a packet from Sergeant Srilk to take up with you. I don't have three days to get it up there."

"Yessir. Who is the receiver?"

He returned his attention to his data sheets. "Just leave it with Private Maxen at supply. Dismissed."

She hesitated a moment. As far as she knew, Trakkas had not once inquired about her capture during the Shon Gat siege. The fact that he was to blame for her even being there didn't seem to bother his conscience. She wanted to ask about the others and perhaps say a few words about Lieutenant Reko, but staring at the top of the major's unevenly shaved head suddenly made her averse to even talk to him. She left without another word.

The air outside was now thick enough with the abrasive dust to force her to pull up her filter cowl to cover her mouth and nose, glad that she had remembered to grab one from the shuttle. The tether's anchor building loomed above the surrounding structures, looking impressive and efficient and, although really little more than a shipping facility, decidedly military. Most of that was due to the armored vehicles, patrols and of course the massive scaffold surrounding the lower part of the tether, studded with communication and surveillance equipment covering the entire hemisphere. The security checkpoint at the entrance was meant to look sleek and elegantly designed but whoever was in charge of the place had by now lost the battle of trying to keep the dust from covering everything. She patted her clothes to add her contribution while the guard checked her credentials and scanned her irises.

The zone beyond the checkpoint looked like a larger version of the elevator hub on the orbiter. The climber loading deck was more tightly guarded and armed guards walked among the rows of containers awaiting shipment. She walked around the hub to a service area and presented the card Major Trakkas had given her.

The clerk glanced at it and then nodded to his left. "Go see Ton Srilk. The Caspian over there."

She nodded and followed his direction. The woman he had pointed out was busy overseeing some sort of repacking of one of the containers. She turned her long, densely furred head when Nova approached. Her yellow eyes were watering even in here. Caspians wore clothes only where custom or policy demanded it but Nova suspected that this one was glad for the coveralls that kept the dust from her intricately patterned hide.

"Sergeant," she said and showed her card again. "Trakkas asked me to pick up a package?"

"And about time," the woman said and dug through her pockets while walking away from the dock workers. "Can't wait to get rid of this."

Nova followed her, baffled by this process and the soldier's lack of manners toward an officer. The Caspian found what she was looking for and slapped a flat metal case into Nova's hand. "Those guys are paid far too well for easy work, if you ask me. Tell Beryl his bag is in—"

"Srilk," a harsh voice barked behind them. Another guard, this one Centauri, glared at her. Nova had no trouble recognizing him as one of Beryl's associates. The last time she had seen him had been with her gun to his throat at Rim Station. "Whiteside," he said. "Moonlighting again? You just can't keep your ass in your Kite, can you, Lieutenant?"

The Caspian's short intake of breath told Nova that a different sort of courier had been expected here today.

"Got to keep things interesting," she said and flipped the container into the air before dropping it into her pocket. "I'll tell Beryl you said hello."

Having no other place to go, Nova walked quickly across the garrison's central square and to the mess hall where she asked for cold tea. Her hand explored the lump in her pocket while she sipped. Payment for what? What was Beryl up to? She frowned, rejecting the idea that he and his men were behind the recent sabotage. They were rotten to the fibers of their pharmaceutically enhanced bodies but they were in this for themselves. She doubted that any of them had the necessary interest or concentration to work for the rebels.

Smuggling was the most likely reason for this payment. If they themselves weren't smuggling goods past the checkpoints, they were allowing shipments to go through uninspected. With Beryl's men in control of security at both the base station as well as the hub on the ranch, doing so was not a difficult feat. And of course Major Trakkas seemed to be in charge of it all, adjusting duty rosters to place his men where they needed to be to keep the goods moving.

Nova tapped her com unit to contact the tower. "Boss, how long till the transport from Siolet arrives?"

"Hours yet, Lieutenant. Still grounded."

Nova considered. Technically, she was on her own right now, with her commanding officer somewhere in orbit. "How's the weather to Rim Station?"

"Clear. Storm's heading west."

Nova signed off, gulped the rest of her tea and hurried to the vehicle depot where she borrowed a skimmer for a trip to visit a friend at her former base. No one seemed to care very much. She remembered to let the clerk at the administrative building know where she was going before jumping into the car and heading out into the flats north of Shon Gat.

An hour of zooming over the barren salt flats brought her to where the base nestled among the foothills. Drab and storm-battered, it resembled any of the Air Command stations on planets like these. If she imagined the dusty ground red, this might be Targon. If she pictured more sand and less rock, it might be K'lar. She pulled into a charging station and left the hangars for the base interior.

"Welcome, Lieutenant," she was greeted by a mechanical attendant at the entrance to the base clinic. Her profile was already displayed in front of the Bellac medic at the main desk when she got there. He greeted her as well but only to inform her that she was not due for an appointment.

"I'm here to see Doctor Soren," she told him. "Could you ask her if she's available, please?"

"I will. Please wait here."

Nova paced around a bit and then stopped to run her hand through a scanner provided for self-assessment. "Ah, I'm Human. Good to know. And indeed a healthy specimen." She slapped the top of the display. "Shots? I'm not due for my shots, you snoop."

"Lieutenant?"

Nova turned.

"Doctor Soren said she can see you for a moment."

Nova smiled politely and followed his direction to the doctor's workspace. Soren came to her feet when Nova entered, a concerned look on her face. "Hello, Lieutenant. I hadn't expected to see you back here so soon. Is... is everything all right?"

"Yes, I'm fine," Nova assured her, realizing that the doctor worried about some lingering effect from her encounter with Captain Beryl. "Everything working as it should. I need to talk to you about something else."

"Oh?" Soren's expression was guarded.

Nova sat down and gestured for the doctor to do the

same. "I want to ask you something about the previous crew here. I think you know who I mean."

"I guess I do." Soren let the door slide shut before taking her chair again.

Nova wondered how to approach this. Now that she was here, the whole thing suddenly seemed a lot more delicate. "I've got reason to suspect that Beryl and his gang are involved in some smuggling at the elevator," she said finally, as so often choosing the most direct route to get to the point. She made a mental note to look up the talented gossip at the ranch to find out how to start conversations with non-coms.

Soren said nothing for a moment. She looked out of the window, thoughtfully tugging on the purple tips of her white hair. "What do you want me to add to that?" she said finally.

"What you know about it."

"I can't."

"You won't?"

"Maybe."

Nova sighed, having half expected this. "I think they're smuggling *mince*. I'm pretty sure they're using it, too."

Soren frowned. "What else would you smuggle out of this place? Half of his thugs are chewing that garbage. Makes things hurt less and it obscures the rest of the dope they use when I test them. The sort that I have to report or the system will do it for me."

"What else are they using?"

She shrugged. "You don't get to be that size without some help. Certainly not the Centauri. They're not built for carrying around all that muscle. They didn't get it from me, if you're wondering."

"I'm here to ask about the *mince*. I'm guessing they're smuggling the stuff up to the station and from there onto commercial ships heading elsewhere."

"It's much bigger than that. They're just paid off to look the other way when the shipments arrive. To make sure they're not searched for contraband. Believe me, the best present Major Trakkas ever got was when General Ausan moved the whole outfit to the elevator. Before that they only had the supply ships that came by here."

"Could they be gun running as well?"

Soren shook her head. "I can't picture it. I can't think of a life form lower than those men but they look down upon rebels as the scourge of the galaxy. They live to destroy them and take pleasure in finding interesting ways to do that. Beryl's squad doesn't take prisoners. The only reason to smuggle guns is to get them to the rebels. They'd never consider that."

Nova nodded. "And Major Trakkas is steering this whole thing?"

"He takes a cut but he lets Beryl do the work. It's why he let them hound you off the base."

"Because of who I am. Because of my father," Nova said, mostly to herself. "They didn't think I'd bend."

"Probably. Not like some of us."

Nova looked into Soren's face, seeing little more than shame there. She leaned forward and placed her hand on the woman's arm. "You can help to stop this," she said urgently. "I have some proof, but not enough. I can't just point a finger and hope Beryl doesn't break my leg for in retaliation. You can come forward and tell what you know. What you've seen."

"Including what he did to you?"

"Yes. Including that. This isn't just about smuggling. It's about people getting hurt if they get in the way. We can't let this happen. Not in the Air Command that I want to work for." Djari's angry face passed briefly through her mind. "This is the sort of thing that makes people distrust the Union. Hate Air Command presence."

"What proof do you have?"

Nova reached into her pocket for the parcel she was to deliver. "I'm guessing that's payment in here. Maybe instructions, messages they can't broadcast. Trakkas told me to take this up to the station. The woman who gave it to me let a few things slip about where it's going."

"So?" Soren smiled sadly. "Trakkas will have a million reasons for whatever he's doing. They've been in this for a long time." She took the box and stood up to run it through an analyzer without opening its seal. "No organics. No dope in there."

"Trakkas has no reason to send money up to the orbiter unless it's pretty damn personal. We don't deal in hard currency, if that's what's in there."

"Maybe it's a pretty bauble for his girlfriend. Even if it isn't, he'd find a way to make sure that's *your* dope. Or *your* money. You have nothing." She looked over the results of the scan again. "The only DNA on that thing is yours. I don't even see a Caspian on that."

"She wore gloves." Nova recalled taking a curious glance at the woman's six-fingered hands. "Can we tag the box somehow? That way we can trace it to Beryl after I deliver it to supply."

Soren laughed. It was a brittle, cold sound. "This is a clinic, not a Prime Staff lair full of gadgetry and dark schemes. Leave the spying to the agents, Lieutenant. Go to your CO. If you need to expose this, tell him what you suspect and walk away."

"Is that what you're doing?" Nova said softly. "Walking away?"

"Yes," Soren said, equally subdued. "Because the things that'll happen to you if Beryl is even just questioned are not something I want visited upon me."

* * *

It was not the best of moods that accompanied Nova as she left Rim Station and headed back into the flats. She flew manually, mulling over Soren's words and very clear warning. The only thing accomplished here was to update her immunization shots, leaving her with a throbbing arm and another reason to have visited the base. She doubted that anyone had even noticed her absence.

She watched the rocky ground pass silently beneath her vehicle as she raced over a landscape too lacking in interest to distract her from her thoughts. Was Soren right? Was staying out of the fray it once again the best option? Avoid getting hurt again? Certainly, the doctor was right in that Nova had little evidence for her accusations. Vague mumblings from a stranger, her assertion that Beryl was impaired while on duty, some orders from a superior officer that weren't entirely protocol. So what?

And what if more people were involved? What about Dakad? What about the station master in charge of the shipping traffic? There was no way to know. Perhaps Djari was right, all along.

Nova's eyes shifted to the horizon when she thought about Djari. His work took him down into the shipping level as new supplies for the grow rings arrived daily. Was he aware of something going on? Perhaps he had seen something, heard something that would offer more evidence.

She brought the skimmer to a halt so abruptly that it nearly crashed the short distance to the ground instead of settling gently according to its design. She opened the canopy and leaped out of the plane, pacing away only to turn around to pace back again.

Djari! She recalled his unheard conversation with Beryl in the corridor. What about that trip to the surface he had not bothered to mention and that his supervisor knew nothing about? Those boxes in his room? With all the equipment available in the grow rings, why would he clutter up his quarters with those analysis tools? Nova leaned against the skimmer, feeling her stomach churn. Could it be? Djari a smuggler? Djari as part of that miserable gang of louts?

So stupid! Nova glared into the direction of the distant elevator, invisible in the haze above the flats. She wanted to storm up there right this very minute to confront him with what she had found. She wanted to shout and rail at him for disparaging the Union's ethics while all along playing his own games. She swore loudly and in several languages, her voice unheard in the empty afternoon desert.

Most of all, she wanted him to deny all of it and show her that none of this was true. Maybe all of this was just a series of coincidences, a chain of small events that really didn't fit together.

But what did she really know about him? Nothing at all. They had shared a few difficult days together and she had been swept away by good looks and a concerned face like some little greenie fresh out of the academy.

A buzzing sound from the skimmer's console interrupted her furious rumination to alert her to the perimeter alarm. She leaned into the vehicle to see what approached, likely a caravan or perhaps an Air Command patrol. Instead, she saw two skimmer sleds closing in from the direction of the base, their destination unmistakably this very spot.

"This is Lieutenant Whiteside to approaching traffic," she said, sounding even to herself like someone not in a mood for company. "Identify yourselves immediately."

There was no reply.

She set her skimmer in motion and veered toward the rolling hills to the east, not surprised when the two other vehicles changed their course as well. Bandits, likely, roaming the flats in search of anyone stupid enough to be out here on their own instead of joining a caravan. But was it possible that Trakkas had sent someone to waylay her? She coaxed more speed out of her machine but a glance at her sensors showed that the skimmers behind her were faster.

She was now heading directly toward the edge of the flats. Hiding herself and the skimmer was not possible with both the vehicle and her com band quite clearly broadcasting her location. Her pursuers were still lost to the distant haze but they drew nearer with each second that passed. "Son of a leprous Rhuwac," Nova cursed. "And you, too, Dakad. Could have sent Sulean. But, no, you had to send Whiteside. And Whiteside had to get nosy. Stupid, stupid—"

Something landed just off her skimmer's port side and exploded in a cloud of dust and sand. Whatever they were lobbing at her from the distance, although not terribly accurate, was sure to stop her skimmer, if not flatten it entirely.

Another burr from her sensors showed more life forms ahead. "Enough already!" she shouted. But these were scattered and there were no power signatures among them. Likely, a caravan bedded down for the night at the edge of the desert.

Without thinking much about the likely outcome of her unformed plan, she entered a new course into the vehicle's systems, working with little more than the view of the hills in front of her. Quickly, she unclipped a gun from beneath the console and then dropped her data sleeve to the floor of the skimmer. Slowing only enough to avoid a broken neck, she retracted the canopy and vaulted to the ground where she tumbled wildly, endlessly until she fetched up against a rock.

Nova lay still, ignoring the pain from whatever damage she had sustained, her attention only on the skimmer. It followed her program to veer south and accelerate toward the rock formations ahead. It was soon out of sight and then Nova heard the distant roar as it crashed into the rocks.

She scrambled to her feet, daring to test her limbs for breaks and sprains, finding nothing more serious than a twisted ankle. "Where is the damn gun!" she shouted, looking around. It had spun from her hand when she leaped from the car and was now nowhere in sight. She decided to ignore the blood on her arms and knee and limped toward where she thought the caravan had stopped. Her pursuers would soon realize that she was not in the crashed skimmer, depending on how much fuel had to burn out before they could check the wreckage.

She fumbled her way through the boulders and scrub, painfully aware that her career choice had made her reliant on sensors and guidance systems. Her standard training in more primitive navigation was ridiculously inadequate for wandering around the plains of Bellac. Trying to remember if Bellac's tusked, meat-eating and much-dreaded *owgs* roamed as far west as this desert didn't make her feel much better about being out here. She stopped to calm her breathing and to listen for the approaching sounds of the sleds.

Fortunately, the nomads weren't concerned about concealment out here. The mournful bellows and bleats of their animals revealed the way to their camp. Nova pushed forward and reached the edge of a herd ambling around the meager scrubland. She sprinted toward one of the churries lolling in the sand. A startled herder moved aside when she lifted the beast's front paw and slipped into the sandy wallow below.

She lay quietly, hoping that the animal, unaccustomed to her, would not decide to evict her. Breathing through the fabric of her sleeve to filter the dust and the churry's aroma, she waited, listening for nearby voices. Soon, she made out the muffled vibration of a skimmer's thrusters through the ground. It stopped.

She flinched at the sound of projectile weapons. It was followed by a clamor of panicked animal grunts and bellows and then the ground shook with the thunder of hooves. Only her sheltering churry remained, apparently trained to stay on the ground when someone lay beneath it. Surely a convenience but now it served only to point out her hiding spot. She felt it tremble.

A long moment later the animal finally rose and shuffled aside. Nova turned onto her back and then slowly came to her feet to face the two Centauri looming over her, both dressed as civilians. She did not recognize either of them. Their guns, however, were of military issue as were the two nearby skimmers.

She looked to her right and left to see the nomads silently approaching from the direction of their camp to investigate the cause of the stampede. They looked like thin, ghostly figures of dun-colored cloth in a dun-colored landscape. Most covered their dyed hair with a burnoose worn against the drifting sands and she did not see their faces. They moved warily, as if waiting to see what would happen here today.

"What do you want," Nova said to her pursuers, doing her best to sound belligerent.

One of the Centauri grasped her arm to pull her toward their vehicles. She moved defensively, drawing on years of close combat training to escape the man's grip. She got free but he simply raised a fist and slammed it into the side of her head. She stumbled and dropped to her knees.

The response to that was immediate. The nomads surged forward like a silent drift of dusty rags and pointy weapons to force the Centauri away from Nova. Her assailants staggered back, arms and weapons raised in surprise as much as surrender. They were forced to the ground and Nova waited for the sound of fists and the screams of pain. None of that happened. Instead, the nomads withdrew after a while, having stripped the men nearly bare of anything even remotely valuable or useful. For one of them that meant a pair of expensive leather trousers.

The Bellacs waited, weapons poised, while the Centauri scrambled to their feet and returned to their skimmers, cursing and glowering but not inclined to linger. One of them shoved aside a young nomad who was busy raiding the skimmer's storage compartment. They departed in the direction of Shon Gat.

Hands reached out to pull Nova from the sand. She let them, crying out when someone gripped her abraded elbow. A searing pain in her foot told her that something wasn't quite right on that end of her body, either.

She was made to sit on a rough-spun blanket and someone gave her a drink so strongly fermented that she nearly gagged. After a moment she took another sip, grateful for the soothing heat that spread through her limbs. A young man with long braids dyed an earthy red took her arm and smeared her wounds with a thick, gritty paste. Nova shook her head in disbelief when she realized that both the drink and the salve were made from the cactus also used to make *mince*.

Others sat nearby, watching silently while the herders strolled off to retrieve the scattered animals. Nova returned their curious gaze, never having been among a tribe of nomads. Union soldiers were not the most popular visitors to Bellac but the plains people were not known to be hostile toward them. Living in this harsh desert had taught them to make the best of both rebel and colonist presence.

An older woman, this one with green tufts of short hair and wearing a gown that had probably been fashionable in Siolet many years ago, reached out and poked a gnarled finger at Nova's insignia. Her long nails were yellowed and thick and resembled claws. "You're an officer," she decided.

"Yes."

"They, too?" The nomad showed Nova one of their new prizes, an Air Command data sleeve. It was a basic com unit without security access or identification.

"Looks that way." Nova watched two nomads admire each other's newly acquired duster and leather pants. "You're well-armed."

"As it must be. Now we're armed even better." The woman laughed, her voice rough with age and desert grit, and pulled the Centauri's rail gun from beneath her once-stately dress.

Nova joined the laughter. By the deep wrinkles around some of the other nomads' eyes visible above their wraps, it was clear that the others were also amused. It seemed that, instead of a caravan of traders and herdsmen, she had stumbled upon a pack of desert bandits. She was untroubled by the distinction. "I need to get to Shon Gat."

"Your plane is broken."

"I'm afraid so." Nova looked around the camp and saw a dilapidated skimmer among the wagons. "Does that thing work?"

"Well enough."

Nova reached into her pocket and withdrew Trakkas' package. Having those men sent after her had added a whole new dimension to things today. Perhaps this thing held some answers. "Do you have something sharp? A blade?"

The matriarch beckoned one of the other nomads who produced a ferocious-looking dagger.

Nova took it gingerly, not without first admiring its design. The handle was a traditional carving although the blade itself was bartered from an off-world supplier. Carefully, she sliced into the seal on the box, aware that those around her were as curious as she was about its contents.

"Well, now we know," she said when the broken case revealed colored and etched metal rods bound with tape. Her new companions exclaimed in wonder at the currency but it meant little to Nova. As Soren had said, a stack of money was proof of exactly nothing. Disappointed, she held the sticks out to the woman. "Will this buy me a quick ride back to the garrison?"

"And dinner, if you wish." The Bellac showed her few remaining teeth. The rods, like her gun, disappeared into the depths of her gown. "Every day for the rest of the wind months."

Nova decided that churry would not be on her menu today. She came to her feet, happy to find her ankle more or less in working order. "No, I need to get back fast."

After enduring a cup of oily tea that was not to be refused, the nomads tinkered with the skimmer until it started up. The vehicle chugged away from the camp on thrusters so misaligned that the man at the controls had to correct its course continually to keep it from tipping. But it moved at a decent speed and the perimeter scan worked, even if its protective dome was long gone and Nova had to avail herself to one of their dense head-coverings to shield her face. Another Bellac rode behind them, legs dangling over the back end, a rifle held across his chest. They left her at the edge of the garrison with a wave and a smile. She looked after them for a moment before limping to the gate.

She stayed within view of the buildings along the entrance into the base and was soon met by several surprised soldiers and ground personnel. She exaggerated her limp and allowed them to usher her to the small hospital, a place she had hoped to never visit again.

Major Trakkas burst into the room, ignoring the medics' protests as he strode to the table where she was still being patched up. "What the hell happened, Whiteside?" he thundered.

She lowered the cooling pad from her lip and stared at him, wide-eyed. "It was terrible, sir! Bandits! I was on the way back from visiting Sergeant Rander and the others at Rim Station when they hit. Out of nowhere! Not a single patrol in hailing distance. I bailed just in time before my skimmer went down."

He glared at her and she practically saw the gears turning in his head. "The package?" he said finally, very quietly.

"Went up with the skimmer. I'm so sorry, sir. But don't worry; those brigands probably didn't get their hands on it. Was it important?"

"No," he said and forced a smile. "It's nothing that can't be replaced. We're all glad you escaped those pirates. I think it's best if you stayed with us overnight, though."

"Thank you, sir. I appreciate your concern." Nova swung her legs over the edge of the stretcher and put her feet on the floor. She reached up to twist her hair into a knot, mainly to hide a grimace of pain when the stretched muscle in her foot agreed with the major. "I'm perfectly fine. Colonel Thedris is expecting me to return promptly with the pilots." She was certain that Thedris had no idea who was piloting the shuttle, if he even knew it was down here. She beamed at Trakkas and directed a meaningful glance at the nearby medic. "I would appreciate if your depot could spare a fresh uniform, though. I'm a complete mess."

His eyes narrowed even as he nodded his agreement. "Of course."

She stood up and found that her foot was likely to cooperate until she got to the shuttle and on her way back to the ranch. If she could manage to get there without finding herself alone somewhere with one of Beryl's thugs, she might even end this day in her own bed behind a locked door.

And then perhaps figure out what to do with the information she had. Most importantly, she had a few questions for Djari.

TEN

By the time Nova delivered her passengers to the skyranch she was utterly weary, stiff from her tumble in the desert and wondering why she had gotten herself so worked up about a gang of thugs and smugglers. She settled the shuttle into its cradle and waited for the air lock to do its thing, wishing she could fall asleep right here.

Soren was right. That one thought had wandered around her mind since leaving Bellac's atmosphere. Keeping her mouth shut about all this would have been the healthiest option. Smuggling was an inevitable part of any shipping port on any planet, Union-owned or not. Was she so driven to seek revenge on Beryl that she'd risk not only her own neck but Soren's as well? And now, instead of acting oblivious to that Caspian's careless comments about payment to Beryl, she was a fresh target walking the halls of Skyranch Twelve. The message she got before the nomads intervened was all too clear. No doubt, news of the failed chase across the flats had preceded her to the orbiter.

The only way to escape more and perhaps permanent damage was to go directly to Lieutenant Colonel Thedris with what she knew, with or without a witness or anything resembling proof. And ask to transfer off the station to avoid floating out in space without a pressure suit before morning.

But first she would give Djari a chance to put her mind at ease.

Could he really be part of this? Or was it possible that he had fallen victim to Beryl's unchallenged intimidation of those around him? Djari's connection to the needs of the grow rings would easily allow him to bring the drug in as part of his shipments of plant material. Mince would appear as organic on the security scanners and, thanks to the other half of the gang on the ground, not deeply scanned for precisely what type of organics.

Once her passengers had cleared out, Nova signed the ship over to the technicians and headed toward the lifts. Before her fingers touched the keyplate the door slid aside and two uniformed Centauri stepped out of the elevator. She recoiled when she recognized Beryl's men.

One of them, a sergeant named Rafe, smirked when he saw her. "Lieutenant Whiteside. We were just coming to welcome you home."

She looked around. "I'm not sure that welcomes are required. I'm familiar with the place."

"Well, the boss sent us to find you. We've been looking all over. He wants a word with you."

Nova felt her heart jump in her chest. No doubt Trakkas had given Beryl some very firm orders about her immediate future. "What boss?"

"Lieutenant Colonel Thedris. How many bosses do you have?"

"The colonel doesn't even know I exist. Why didn't he just call me?"

The Centauri pointed at her forearm, still missing the data sleeve she had dropped in the skimmer before it blew. "A little hard to find without your com. So he asked us to take a look around."

His companion nudged her not too gently toward the lift. "And he seems to be in a hurry for that to happen."

"I'll go see him right away," she said. "After I get a fresh uniform. I just got back from the surface. Tell him I'll just be a few minutes."

The Centauri guards crowded her into the elevator that simply did not seem built for men of their size. Rafe let his eyes wander over her body for a thoughtful moment. "That uniform looks just fine to me."

Nova swallowed the ugly lump of fear that rose in her throat. The soldiers stood too close to her. She could feel them, smell them. Her every instinct and every bit of training and experience told her to flee. There was no colonel waiting for her. There was only Beryl and these thugs, ready to silence her permanently in some entertaining fashion. She recalled Djari's comment about the usefulness of fear. She beat it down, little by little, as the lift rose toward the upper levels. "I mean it. I don't want to be seen by Thedris like this. It'll just take a moment."

"We'll come with you," Rafe offered. "Just to make sure you don't get lost."

"Are you arresting me, then, Sergeant?" she snapped, grateful when her words came out firm. Without waiting for his response, she changed the destination of the lift to stop two floors below the administrative level. With luck, some of the pilots were loitering around there as they sometimes did before hitting the lounge for a late-evening drink. "Because unless you are, I can find my room on my own."

Both men stepped out of the lift when she did. The hallway was deserted and no one lounged around the common area near the arched windows. Nova took a few steps toward her quarters, spun around again and leaped into the lift just as its door closed. She punched the controls for the floor below, praying to the gods of Bellac that the other lift was on a distant level.

She squeezed out of the car before the doors had fully opened and raced down the corridor. She passed one, two sub-sections of residential units before slapping her hand against the keyplate of one door among many. It slid aside and she stumbled into Djari's room with a loud sob of relief.

She pressed her mouth and nose into her elbow to muffle

the sound of her deep gasps for air, out of breath with fear and exertion. She leaned against the door, listening to the menacing thump of combat boots. They grew louder, then passed. Then stopped. Rough voices murmured something too low to make out. The footfalls returned and then faded again.

Nova closed her eyes and tipped her head back against the door. Now what? Where was Djari? Working late? Or was he down at the docks, perhaps, packing up the latest shipment of dope? The bed was unmade, which wasn't all that unusual, and once again he had left his com band on the table beside it. But the room wasn't just empty of boyfriend but also empty of the stacks of boxes he had stashed here. None on the floor, none on the unused bunk. She now had a fairly reasonable guess as to what had been in them.

She picked up his com band and idly turned it over in her hands when a terrible thought struck home. Had Beryl's men harmed Djari? Did they know about her involvement with him? She looked around the room again as if in search of a splatters of blood or some sign of a struggle. Was she the leverage they were using to get him to cooperate?

It would work, of that she was certain. Neither of them had indulged in breathless declarations of love and dedication during their magnificent bouts of lovemaking but they both knew the possibility was there. She needed his serenity as much as he craved her passion. He would go far to keep her from harm. It was also the reason she had not told him that it was Beryl who had assaulted her at Rim Station. She had no doubt that he cared for her deeply. What was a bit of smuggling to keep her safe? He had little to lose up here.

Nova looked around for something to use as a weapon, should Rafe still roam the halls. Feeling a little uneasy about looking through Djari's things, she peered into some of the cabinets. Most held untidy stacks of clothes and work coveralls. But when she opened a bin near the door her breath caught. A rail gun, fully charged. A small projectile weapon and cases of bullets. A precision laser tool not usually employed by botanists. With a silent curse at finding yet more hints about his new career choice, she took the projectile weapon and tucked it into her uniform blouse.

She went to the door and pressed her ear against it. Someone, distantly, was singing off-key and joyfully. Taking a deep breath, she opened the door and peered outside. Empty. It was only a few seconds to the lifts.

But instead of directing the car to the administrative level and the colonel's office, she dropped it to the shipping floor. She had to know for sure. She had to see. Somewhere down there was the evidence she needed. She was also sure that somewhere in the back of her mind she hoped that there was nothing to be found at all.

The hallway outside the restricted area was silent. She listened to the heavy tread of boots to warn her of the guards' approach. When she heard nothing but the muffled sounds of industry behind these walls, she stole along the corridor to the unfinished passenger lift Djari had shown her. It was still unlocked and she slipped inside and then climbed the ladder to the catwalk. The stairless gap in the wall showed her a view of the elevator hub, looking much like the last time she had seen it. Workers, supervisors, but no armed guards tonight. Were they all out looking for her?

She did not resist the pull of the shimmering stars outside and stopped to remember the moments she and Djari had shared here. Perhaps she was avoiding what she had come here to see. Turning her back to the stars, she went to the corner of the secret space and pulled one of the bins into the light. It was sealed but unlocked, marked by customs agents as cleared. She broke the seal wire and slid the lid aside.

And found coil upon coil of *mince*.

Nova closed her eyes for a moment. When she opened them again, the stuff was still there. She slipped her hand down along the inside of the tub to feel more of them and encountered something hard and smooth. Pushing the coils aside exposed an opaque bottle, tapered at the ends, without markings and likely a liquid form of the drug. Quickly, she closed the bin and pushed it back into the corner to pile another on top to hide the broken seal. There was nothing left to do now but to find someone who was not on Trakkas' pay sheet and reveal what she had found. One of the other pilots, perhaps. Rolyn, surely, would stand by her. And then it was most definitely time to see the colonel.

She hurried back down to the corridor and had just pulled the door shut when someone in stained coveralls turned the corner, carrying a container like the ones she had seen above. She froze and he froze and both of them stared at each other for a moment before he dropped the box and ran.

"Hey!" she called after him, surprised by his escape. She raced after him down the hall leading to the lifts. If he ducked into a restricted entrance on this level the chase would end quickly. Nova's daily and strenuous exercise routines served her well and she soon caught up to the Bellac. When he sprinted past the elevator doors and to a short staircase she launched herself over the railing and pulled him to the floor. She had straddled him, her gun to his throat before he had even realized what had happened.

He squeezed his eyes shut and spread his arms out in defeat. "Don't shoot. Please, Lieutenant!"

She let him cringe for a moment while catching her breath. "Why did you run?"

He opened his eyes slowly, one at a time. The network of veins normally visible on a Bellac's neck had turned a deep purple with the exertion of the chase. "Because you have a gun?"

She jabbed him with the barrel. "It was holstered. Again, why did you run? You were taking the box up to the stash, weren't you?"

"Please don't turn me in, Lieutenant. I'm just doing what I'm told."

"Told by whom?"

He shook his head. "No, please. I can't."

"You have no choice."

"No. Shoot me now. I don't care. Better that than… *that.*"

"Than what?" She shifted away from him and gestured with the gun for him to sit on the bottom stairs. The foot she had injured down on Bellac throbbed steadily after her dash to catch this man. "Talk to me or we're both going topside right now."

Again, he shook his head. "I can't. I have kids. Two girls. Here on the station."

"He threatened your children?"

"I didn't say that. But things happen. You know about that accident when one of the deck hands fell off the upper scaffolding?"

She nodded.

"That's not how she broke her neck."

"They are murdering people now?" Nova gasped.

"There were others. I won't be one of them. I just do what I'm told and get to go home to my girls at night."

"Names. Just nod. Beryl?"

His eyes darted around the hallway before he nodded.

"Vel Ancel? Tajana?"

Again, the nod.

She wavered for a few seconds before asking: "Nathon Djari?"

"Who? No, don't know that one."

"Human, works in the rings. Scar on the side of his face."

"Seen him around. But he never talked to me. Is he one of them?"

Nova put her gun away and pulled him to his feet. "Look. These people have to be stopped. You can help stop them. Tell the colonel what you told me."

"I told nothing!" he said and moved ahead of her back up the stairs.

"This is going to come out sooner or later," she tried. "Is this worth losing your job over? Maybe going to prison?"

He turned back, angry now. "It's not worth losing my life over. What do I care what gets smuggled through here?"

"People are dying over this!"

"Only the ones that don't mind their own business. I'm doing well so far."

"Living in fear?"

He stared at her and his mouth formed words that didn't quite make it past his lips.

She touched his arm, again astonished by the power Beryl wielded over these people. "Tell no one you saw me. You can at least do that, can't you? Just clear out. Go home to your girls. You don't want to be here when we get back."

He nodded wordlessly and stumbled away, perhaps to retrieve the box he had dropped.

Nova returned to the lift and directed it to the administrative level. Pointlessly, she tried to straighten her hair and uniform in the reflection of the elevator's wall. She looked like some lunatic about to storm into her commanding officer's presence with tales of drug smuggling and extortion. With luck, her so-far spotless record would convince the colonel to at least come down here to see the evidence for himself.

She felt calm and resolute by the time she stepped out of the car and onto the elegantly designed upper floor of the station. Her calm and resolution flew out of the graphene re-enforced windows when she saw Rafe. He, Ancel and two others of Beryl's security team stood at the entrance of the vast workspace shared by the administrators of the skyranch.

This time there was no sardonic smirk to welcome her. She walked toward them as if in some sort of nightmare. The men, three Centauri and a Human, seemed like alien creatures in their ill-used, armored uniforms and well-kept weapons, covered in tattoos and scars and a cloud of ill will. In contrast, even at this hour teams of well-groomed individuals worked quietly up here, separated by invisible sound proofing, politely oblivious to the lower-level ruffians among them.

"Whiteside," Rafe said. "Finally decided to report to the colonel?"

She frowned. Had he actually told the truth when they had come for her? What would the station commander want with her at this hour? True, he was temporarily their wing commander as well but so far had left those duties to the other officers, relying heavily on his squadron leaders.

She walked silently past the grunts to look around the vast space. Indeed, she saw the colonel near the terrace in conversation with several officers. She stopped by a receptionist who directed her into a separate area, this one with opaque walls and furnished with a few lounges and chairs. She sat stiffly near the door.

Two of the guards followed her. Ancel leaned against the wall, so close to her that his hip brushed her arm. She rose from her seat and moved to another. Rafe flung himself into a deep armchair and, out of sight of the staff in the main work space, propped his boot against the back of another.

"So what did our favorite pilot do to get an audience with the big boss," he said.

"How would I know?"

"Could it be that you have something to tell him?"

"Not your business, is it?"

"Maybe it is. Had a little trouble down on Bellac earlier?"

"No. Why?"

He leered up at Sergeant Ancel. "Where's that blond boyfriend of yours these days?"

She tried to ignore him but found that she could not. "What did you do to him? How did you get him to cooperate?"

He shrugged, making it clear that he had too much fun in keeping her wondering. "He didn't take much convincing. Humans are weak. They scare easy." He leered at her. "Not like you, though, Nova."

"Lieutenant Whiteside," she corrected.

"By the time Beryl's had his say with the colonel, you'll be lucky to be Private Whiteside. Do you really think that we don't have this covered? That some snoop like you actually matters?"

"I do think that. You wouldn't be up here threatening me if you weren't scared green."

He shook his head but it seemed to her that some of the sneering arrogance had left his unshaven face. "Beryl tells us you spread for him like a blanket." He placed his hand on his groin and left it there. "Is that true, Nova? He said you had some decent parts on you."

"You'll never know," she said, sure of his bluff now that nothing remained but lewd suggestions with the threat of more violence.

"We'll see. Guess you haven't had a nice piece of Centauri before."

She regarded him coolly. "Well, I have. Although that one liked to bathe."

Ancel, still slouching by the door, cackled with laughter when Rafe scowled at her. He sat up straighter in his chair when a woman in a stylish sky-colored wrap came to the door. She did not look at him but gestured to Nova with a polite smile and an impossibly delicate hand.

Nova stood up. She bent slightly toward Rafe as she passed. "It's called soap, *shekka'an*. Write that down somewhere so you don't forget."

It felt odd to walk past people speaking to each other and yet not hear a word through the discreet sound baffles. She stepped through one of those shields onto the open terrace overlooking the lower levels, waiting to be called. Even at this hour, a few off-duty staffers were enjoying the space. A nice place to take a late meal, she thought, feeling her stomach rumble despite her apprehension.

"Lieutenant Whiteside," she heard finally from some hidden sound source. "Please join us."

She looked up to see the station commander gesture to her from his workspace further along the terrace. Nearby stood Captain Dakad and a crisply uniformed Feydan major whom she did not recognize. She fought an irrational urge to run away.

"Sir." She saluted the officers and stood stiffly before

them.

"Whiteside," the colonel indicated a seat close to him. There was no table between them and she sat awkwardly, crossing and then uncrossing her legs. Her boots were caked with desert dust and she tucked them under the chair.

Thedris held a data unit in his hand. He regarded her for a long while and she berated herself for not having taken a minute to at least put on a set of fatigues instead of remaining in this rumpled uniform. She glanced at Dakad and saw nothing helpful there.

The colonel looked down at his screen. "Your records," he informed her. The officer seemed relaxed, his formal jacket unfastened, the shock of black hair casually brushed over the crown of his head. The light from above reflected eerily in his eyes when he looked up again. "I've had the pleasure of working with Colonel Tegan Whiteside once. Outstanding officer."

"Yessir."

"From what I see here, you look to be following his example."

"I try, sir. Thank you."

"Forty hours left until your Hunter Class trials. Impressive. What is your goal after that?"

She lifted her chin. "Targon, sir."

He raised an eyebrow. "A fine objective, Lieutenant. That'll put you on a battleship into deep space."

"I hope so, sir."

"Much more interesting than guarding this dust ball." He pointed down, toward the planet. "Or patrolling a jumpsite."

"Those assignments have their challenges as well," she replied dutifully.

He nodded. "You've lost some colleagues recently. I'm sorry. That is never easy."

"No, sir. They'll be missed. Our squad was... is a tight unit."

He looked up at Dakad. "That is good to hear."

She glanced at the Feydan major standing beside the

colonel. She stood with one hand around the wrist of the other, no doubt recording this meeting with the camera in her data sleeve. Her elaborately tattooed face gave nothing away. She and Dakad would also be sitting if any of this was as informal as the colonel appeared. Nova stopped herself from squirming nervously as she tried to recall anything that might give her cause to feel as nervous as she did. Nothing came to mind.

"As you know, we're still involved in the investigation of the horrific event on the flight deck. It appears that a new material was used to compromise the power packs on General Ausan's shuttle. We've traced some components to Pelion so far."

She frowned. "Those packs aren't volatile. What we saw was an explosion."

"Exactly. The labs are busy figuring that out."

"Sabotage, then? Rebels?"

"Likely. The question is: how did it get aboard?"

"I'm sorry, sir. That isn't my field. I would assume the material was already aboard her cruiser when it arrived."

He tipped his head. "A reasonable assumption. Leaving the entire Siolet base under suspicion."

"I suppose," she said uncomfortably. "Some of us were guessing that they wanted to blow it here to make a statement about the orbiter. And bag a few pilots while at it."

"Also reasonable. Meaning that someone up here could have tampered with those packs after the general arrived." He gestured to the terraces. "Crew, admin, pilots."

"Sir, surely you're not suggesting that the pilots had anything to do with this. Our pilots suffered as many casualties as the ground crew." She leaned forward, unable to hold herself in check much longer. "Why am I being questioned? And here? By you?"

"The rest of the station staff is being interviewed by security. But we have some additional inquiries for you."

"Sir?"

"Tell us about Djari Nathon," he said, watching her

intently.

"Djari?"

He consulted his screen for the correct name. "That's Nathon Lis Djari. You know him well."

Nova blinked, trying to discern the direction of this inquisition. "Yes. He was with us in Shon Gat. Working with the wounded there."

"Yes, we're aware of what happened there."

"He... he's a farmer. Somewhere in the Rift. He said he came to look for work up here."

"And you petitioned General Ausan to expedite that."

"Yessir. He showed great fortitude at Shon Gat. He helped us escape. It seemed a small reward for his actions."

"What is your relationship with him now?"

She furrowed her brow. "He's been dealing with some... difficulties. But I like to think that we are friends," she added firmly.

The colonel came to his feet and gestured for her to remain seated when he walked to the perimeter of the sound-shielded space. He looked out over the terrace for a while before returning to stand behind her. She felt him place his hand on her shoulder and fought an urge to pull away.

"Your *friend* is under suspicion of aiding the rebel on Bellac," he said finally.

"What?" she cried out before biting her lip and reminding herself to hold it together in front of these people. "That's not possible."

"Oh?"

"He's suffered as much as any of the locals have. He's no rebel."

"He may be a spy. Or even just a sympathizer."

She shook her head. "He has no regard for them." She looked up at him. "And he would not even think about something as horrific as the sabotage in the hangar. He cares about people. I've seen it."

The colonel returned to his chair, likely assured that they had enough video of her reaction to this news.

"Besides," she said. "If he's a spy he's not a very good one. He's never pushed me for any information that he shouldn't have. And he was hurt in the blast, too."

"He had no business on that deck."

She shrugged. "He said he was picking up a shipment of seeds."

"Five cargo pods arriving daily and he has seeds delivered to the flight hangar? The whole point of the elevator is to make that unnecessary. Security should have stopped him. Yet he seemed to know how to avoid them."

"He's a farmer. What would he know about placing explosives onto a guarded Air Command cruiser?"

"How do you know he's a farmer?"

Nova closed her eyes. Chemical analysis kits in his room. Boxes of material there one day and gone the next. Guns. Evasive answers. "I don't."

"Coria Taren," he said.

"Sir?"

"Coria Taren, liberated along with yourself and a few others at Shon Gat. I'll say that 'liberated' is not the correct word. She is a confessed rebel operative who's been working in Shon Gat for months. She was also 'captive' along with you and Nathon Djari?"

"Yes," Nova said. "I suspected she might have been one of them." She looked up, feeling caged. "I was in no position to arrest her."

"But you did not suspect your friend Nathon Djari?"

"I can't believe he would side with the Shri-Lan." She looked up at Dakad and then stood up to pace, as Colonel Thedris had done, to the edge of the terrace. Crossing her arms she looked up through the skylight to the glittering solar collectors above.

Was it possible? She thought about Djari's endless patience and gentle handling of the injured at Shon Gat. His knowledge of agriculture was undoubtedly the main reason for his presence up here, with or without her recommendation. He had been a solid rock in what had been weeks of turmoil for her, and that only for a few exhausting, confusing days.

But he had not once asked her about Coria. Did he know what happened to her? When he escaped Beryl's men at Shon Gat, was it to flee for his life or to avoid being taken to the garrison? Had the rebels captured him after that, or had he joined them on his own accord? She had heard him rail against the Union and against Air Command methods. She had dismissed it as weary grumblings in a miserable situation.

And maybe, she thought, this was the reason why he had showed so little concern over her flippant comment after he had first made love to her. If the colonel's accusation were true, Djari knew that there was no future here on this orbiter for him and that there was none for them together. At best, she thought, he cared enough to want to stop her from boarding the doomed shuttle. And she had responded by practically flinging herself into his bed.

"Idiot," she whispered. Gullible, unthinking, impulsive, stupid! How she ached to confront him this minute, wherever he might be. She went back to where the others waited, unmoving. "You wouldn't be telling me this if you thought I was compromised, too. What do you want from me?"

Thedris waited until she had taken her chair again. "Normally, I'd relieve you of duty, arrest him and see how the investigation shakes out."

"And abnormally?" she said, too angry and disappointed for military etiquettes.

"I've spoken to your past commander." He peered more closely at his screen. "Andridge on Tannaday. The two tours you did there were well spent. She speaks highly of you. For the most part. Your loyalty to the Commonwealth is not in question."

"I'm glad," she said flatly.

He pursed his lips and shifted them around for a bit as if making up his mind about something before speaking. "You'll continue your friendship with him. None of our agents have been able to get on anything more than a sociable footing with him. He's polite but we get nothing but a blank wall from him."

"You want me to spy for you?"

"Yes. We think he might be able to lead us to more higher-placed rebels in the Bellac Shri-Lan group. Perhaps even outside of Bellac. There is nothing to be gained by arresting him just yet. He's a minor piece. We're not even sure that he was responsible for the explosion in the hangar."

She looked up at Captain Dakad as if for help. "I'm not trained for covert ops."

"We're not sending you into Shri-Lan headquarters." Thedris smiled up at the Feydan major. "Although it would be a day for celebration if you found out where that is these days." His expression sobered when he returned to his screen. "You have enough training in languages, surveillance equipment and security protocol to be useful. We want you to engage him, discover what you can about rebel activities on Bellac or elsewhere."

"Is he dangerous?"

"He's not a farmer."

Nova had to make an effort to maintain her erect posture, wanting nothing so much as wilt in her chair, perhaps with a cozy blanket wrapped around her. Oddly, her thoughts wandered to Lieutenant Boker. Heiko Boker, who would surely come up with some disrespectful comment about this, who would ultimately comfort her with something fairly sensible, and who was dead now. Perhaps because of Djari. How she wished for him now, the only person here, other than Lieutenant Rolyn, to whom she might admit her stupidity for having trusted the man.

"What is he, then?" she said.

"We don't know. He's been in Shon Gat for some time, waiting for a work placement up here. None of the rebels we captured there had any information about him."

"Including Coria?"

"Including her." He observed her for a moment.

"Lieutenant, I can imagine it is difficult to hear that a friend has fallen under suspicion. We all know that saboteurs have been able to infiltrate many levels of both Air Command and Union governance. That doesn't make it easier to find out that a trusted person is not who they appear to be."

She nodded but his words brought a small whisper of hope. "What about our people? Is it possible that he's an agent? One of ours? Working in Shon Gat?"

The colonel shook his head. "We checked with Targon. There are no special ops going on that we weren't aware of. Our own plain clothes are accounted for."

"May I ask why you suspect him? Other than that he's not a farmer?"

The major standing beside Thedris finally found her voice. "As part of the investigation we have been tracing the movements of all station personnel over the past few weeks. Nathon Djari made two trips to the surface to arrange for plant material. In both cases, he met briefly with the growers and then took a private skimmer into Siolet. Accurate facial recognition is very easy right now, given his recent injury. He was spotted in several locations that are known to be sympathetic of Shri-Lan members. He sent coded messages from here to a mobile operative on the surface not long before the explosion. We suspect a receiver hidden among the caravans. A closer examination of his background turned up a number of discrepancies, although artfully concealed. He is now under surveillance."

Nova was still processing the information she had just been given. "Huh? What?"

"We are tracking his movements and have placed surveillance at key points along his daily routine."

"You bugged his room?" she gasped, aware of a furious blush creeping up along her neck. "When?"

"Yesterday. When we received the report from Command."

Nova dared to breathe again, suddenly very skeptical about Djari's motive for taking their private encounters elsewhere on the station. So much for star-dappled poetry! He just wasn't much for having his love life recorded. If he did, indeed, work for the Shri-Lan, checking his room for hidden devices would be routine.

How she wished she still thought of him as just a smuggler! Captain Beryl and his self-serving operation suddenly seemed very insignificant in comparison to these accusations.

"Colonel, I'm not sure I'm comfortable with—"

A strident, pre-emptive whine from the colonel's com system cut her off in mid-sentence. He tapped his sleeve to receive the message without voice. His brow furrowed. Several minutes passed before he closed that communication and began another, this one audible.

"Shri-Lan forces have attacked the Rim Station with a shipment of Rhuwacs," he transmitted. "Shrills are reported over Siolet near the commerce center. A carrier just came out of subspace at the jumpsite and has engaged our fighters out there. All are requesting reinforcements."

Dakad and Nova exchanged a startled look. He tapped his own communicator to sound an alarm in the pilots' quarters and on their com bands. "We're deploying. Pilots only. Not a drill. Upper flight deck in ten."

"Sir, what about the elevator base?" the Feydan Major asked.

"Shon Gat is quiet," Thedris replied and turned to Dakad. "Take your squad to the jumpsite. We'll send Caga down to Siolet."

"Aye," Dakad replied. "You're with me, Whiteside."

ELEVEN

"What's going on at the jumpsite?" Nova asked when she arrived at their rally point, still fastening her flight suit. A glance at the overhead screen showed that the other two squads stationed here were also mobilized. She held a new data sleeve up to let its sensor record her retina and begin to download her programs. "Is everyone deploying?"

"Yes," Rolyn answered. "Dead silent around here. It's all going down at Siolet and the 'site. There's going to be one big rebel ass-kicking when I get out there, I promise you."

They listened to the urgent messages reporting the sudden appearance of one of the Shri-Lan's rare carriers at the jumpsite. A hail of Shrills had descended upon the Air Command ship stationed there, forcing them to scramble both of the local squadrons to protect the partially complete relay station.

"How far out are we?" Nova's screen showed that the planet's position along its orbit put them in fairly easy distance to the jumpsite. They could arrive there within the hour. "You'd think they'd wait until we're elsewhere."

"They're brilliant tacticians," Rolyn said as he pulled his

helmet over his head. "Looks like you'll be collecting a few points today, Whiteside."

"Yeah," she said, but even to herself sounded lacking in enthusiasm. The colonel's accusation buzzed around her head like some annoying insect. She tried to swat it by remembering why she was here. This was about joining her squad and doing her job and maybe dispense a little justice to those who had murdered their friends. "Make sure to say ooh and aah when Dakad can hear it."

"Ladies," Dakad shouted when the displays showed that his squad was assembled and their sections confirmed. "Saddle up. Let's get this furball swept up before they get here. They took out the relay at Callas so who knows what else is coming through that hole."

Nova tapped Rolyn's helmet and rushed for her Kite. Nikki, her favorite hangar jockey, gave her a leg up onto the wing and she slid into her pilot couch with a giddy sense of anticipation that she quickly suppressed. The Kite recognized her neural link when she engaged the interface and the systems came online. Like the others, she would wait until they reached the battlefield before deciding to rebalance the command functions of the plane. Nova preferred to handle her Kite manually and target enemy ships via the mental interface while some of the other pilots did the opposite. She hovered off the ground and listened to the count as each section moved into the chutes and from there into space.

"Section Four is a go," Flight Control announced.

Nova halted outside as she waited for the other two in her section to fall in. "Come on, come on," she said, impatient to be gone. She turned briefly to give a thumbs-up to Rolyn when something far below the flight deck caught her eye. A cruiser attached to the shipping docks seemed strangely out of place there, Those spaces were usually occupied by the boxy transporters that never entered planetary atmosphere as they plied their trade between orbiters and base stations. Occasionally, a cargo ship from outside the system docked there to save the expense of landing. But the ship down there now was a private passenger cruiser of Caspian build, not the class of vessel used by Air Command. Certainly not a vessel meant to haul *anai* oil or frozen fish.

She considered only briefly. If that ship was a smuggler, choosing this moment to remove the *mince* from the station, any evidence she had against Trakkas and his men would be gone. She swooped out from the station and then immediately cut her speed. "Whiteside lame," she said. "Returning to base."

Dakad kept his usual expletive-laden comment to himself. "Shake it out or pick up another plane, Whiteside."

"Heard. Don't wait for me." She circled wide and ran a few tests that would seem legit on sensors while taking a closer look at the shipping docks. "Tower, is there a shipment coming in today? Any type?"

"Affirmative," she heard the harried reply from the tower where everyone was too busy with the remaining launch to worry much about a kink in her wing or questions about shipping. "Are you coming in?"

"Yes." She hovered into a chute on the upper deck. A private cruiser on the shipping level? None of this, including the attacks on the jumpsite or Siolet, felt right. "Do your job, Whiteside," she mumbled even as she slid over her wing and to the ground. "They know what they're doing. You just go shoot some rebels."

"Lieutenant?" Her squad's ground mechanic had come over to where she stood.

"Check the port lifts, Nik. Wagging all over the place."

"Where are you going?"

Nova raised a hand to signal an urgency of a personal nature and dashed off into the direction of the deck's hygiene station. She passed it and, still berating herself for this departure from protocol, entered a lift and dropped to the shipping level.

It was quiet down here. No clanging of transport containers, no shouts, curses or laughter from the work crew.

With the alert, the docks had been cleared of non-essential personnel and only the elevator hub would still be staffed. The security team assigned to patrol these passages was nowhere in sight. If she was right about them, today presented the opportunity to load up the cruiser moored to the locks. Perhaps they had even been aware of the impending Shri-Lan attack.

But was that likely? Trakkas might well be a greedy opportunist but he was also a seasoned Air Command officer. Beryl and his group were crude and pitiless, but each considered himself as the embodiment of soldierhood. Perhaps that included smuggling and even murder but never treason. News of a rebel attack would not go unreported.

Nova hurried to the end of the corridor and slipped through the unmarked door. Instead of climbing the scaffold to the unfinished catwalk, she moved silently down the ladder and onto the floor. There was still not much to be heard but the steady hum of well-designed machinery. The relays feeding electric power down to the planet were green-lighted and the elevator itself was in motion.

She heard voices to her left and slipped into a space between the orderly stacks of bins. Someone hurried past her. He came from the direction of the locks, a cylinder in his hands. She stepped forward again to see where he was going with it, whatever it was.

Then she saw a pair of legs, clad in the cargo hands' orange coveralls, splayed out on the floor. The rest of the body was bent around the edge of the companionway to the main entrance from the station. Beyond him lay someone else, this one unmistakably dead, the upper body crisscrossed with laser burns.

Nova's hand moved to her side only to realize that she was in her flight suit and, appropriately, her gun belt was still back in her quarters. She raised her arm to activate her com unit. "Security, Whiteside—"

The barrel of a gun stabbed below her ear hard enough to bring her teeth down onto the tip of her tongue. A hand shot out to grasp her wrist before she could complete her call. Two people in civilian dress, one Bellac, the other Caspian, dragged her into the open space near the tether. Someone pulled her data sleeve off her forearm and searched her for additional devices.

"Get rid of her," someone nearby said. The voice belonged to a Centauri woman standing near the elevator monitoring station.

"Stop!" another voice, this one much more familiar, rang out.

Nova turned to see Djari rush toward them. He was not wearing the coveralls identifying him as ring crew and the gun at his thigh was also not standard issue.

"Leave her to me," he said. "I'll take care of this." He grasped her arm to pull her away from them.

She twisted out of his grip. "What is this? What are you doing?"

"The question is: what are you doing here? You're supposed to be with your squad."

She looked around. "Is this part of what's happening out there? The attack at the jumpsite? Djari, what is going on?"

He glanced over to his companions. "You have to get out of here, Nova. I never meant for this to happen with you here. Please! There is still time."

"Time for what?" She was suddenly very alarmed by the fear and worry on his face. "I was just told that you're with *them*. With the Shri-Lan. I can't believe that!"

He looked away. "You really had no idea? You never suspected?"

"No! Gods, Djari, I trusted you!" She reconsidered. "Well, I thought maybe you were getting into the smuggling going on here with Beryl's gang. But Shri-Lan? Those animals?"

"Animals? It's your people who are the animals on Bellac, Lieutenant. And that's not being kind to animals. You have destroyed the peace of this planet."

"You wouldn't even be on Bellac if not for the Union,"

she said, not really interested in rebel rhetoric at this moment. She glanced at his gun.

"You'd be dead before you can even touch that," he said with a nod to the nearby rebels who, although out of earshot, were watching intently, weapons poised.

"Why, Djari? Please just tell me."

"I told you why. You don't belong here."

"You're not a rebel. I think I know you better than that. You care too much. I've seen it."

"Don't try that on me, Lieutenant," he said. "Leave the head stuff to the non-coms. But if you have to know I'll tell you that I used to have a family before Air Command came into the Rift. Blew away half the town looking for a rebel depot. My town."

She looked up into his tortured face as he remembered. "I'm so sorry, Djari…"

"So I went to Shon Gat. Maybe to try to figure things out. Met Coria and some others and the things they said sounded right. Then you came and I thought maybe they were wrong." His hand moved to the twisted scar along his cheek. "For a while, anyway. Then I learned more about your precious Air Command than I wanted to know."

She shook her head. "Doesn't have to be like this," she whispered.

"It doesn't?" he said angrily. "You were there! You held torn Bellac guts in your hands, making do without the tools only your people own. How can you still do this!"

"Nearly time, Djari," someone called.

"Time for what?" Nova said to him.

"Time to go."

She looked over to the Centauri at the elevator monitors. The climbers were controlled from the main command station on the admin level but this console dealt with emergencies. "What did you do? Is there going to be an attack on the station?"

"We can't even get close. But we can still take it down."

"What? How? This place is a fortress." Would a scream

from her alert anyone to their presence? The dampening around this area was designed to keep noise levels low. Were there even guards within earshot? Had they also been killed?

"The elevator. The climber is stacked with explosive. The sort that'll blow on impact, like your concussion charges. It's been on its way here for three days. It only has to hit the shields hard enough to detonate. I don't want you here when that happens."

"What?" Nova whispered. She gaped at him in terror and wonder. It would work. The shielding at the tether connection doubled as an emergency brake in case of climber failure. But had anyone considered an impact detonation at precisely that point? A large enough blast could disengage the elevator from the station, sending the ranch into space and, eventually, wrap large swaths of the tether around the planet at terminal velocity, like a whip across the landscape. "That's why you went down to the surface the other day?"

He nodded. "And to make sure it's done right we've got a few bottles of the boom juice up here as well." He gestured toward several clusters of unmarked cylinders piled up near the tether's terminal. "It was easy to figure out what Beryl was up to and get onto his crew. People stupid enough to give me access to this place. And too stupid to realize that dope wasn't the only thing coming up the tether."

Nova groaned. The bins allowed to pass through here without inspection by Beryl's men would also have contained the explosive. Djari's presence here, as a frequent receiver of goods from below, would be unremarkable as he removed his portion of the clandestine shipment.

"And the general? Did you murder her? Did you kill my friends, Djari?"

"No. That charge was set by one of the civilians that came up with her. I tried to get you out of there when I was told about it. I don't want you hurt."

"Listen to yourself! You'd murder hundreds of people up here but you'd feel sorry about me? This is crazy! Please don't do this, Djari. What about those on the surface? This will be terrible for them."

"And a lesson will be learned!" he snapped. He took a deep breath as he looked over to the air lock. "You can come with us, Nova. With me. You can leave all this. There is a better way."

"How can you even ask me this? This is wrong, Djari. You know it's wrong!"

"In the end it won't be. There are always victims in a war. And this is a war, even if you choose to call us rebels." He held his hand out to her. "Please come with me. I care about you. I want you with me. You matter."

"You lied to me," she said. Where was security? Did no one realize that there was something very wrong going on down here?

"You're right to feel... betrayed, I guess. Once all this started I didn't want you to get involved with this. But I wanted you so bad. You're so... I just wanted..." He ran his hand through his hair, looking for just a moment like the man who had caught her attention and her heart in the slums of Shon Gat. "I'm sorry it went this far. I should have stayed away from you."

"Djari, dammit," one of his cohorts called. "We're done. Let's get out of here!"

"You can still stop this," she whispered urgently. "Shut down the elevator. Please!"

"Not possible. The com link to the climber is down. The relay is recoded so the command center won't notice. Nor will ground control. There are no brakes on that thing now. When it gets here it's going to crash. We'll take you away with us. I want you to live, Nova."

Before she could reply, something large and dark and flying through the air drew their attention. The object landed with a thud among them and they all saw that it was the body of a Centauri. Everyone looked up to see four Union soldiers along the catwalk above them, guns aimed.

The rebels scattered at once, fleeing into the stacks where more soldiers awaited them. Laser fire lit up the air as the tracers found their targets. Nova spun and ran into a row of waiting shipping containers near the locks. She squeezed through a gap too narrow for Djari and headed for the doors. The overhead lights had turned orange as the rest of the station was alerted to a security problem.

She stumbled and fell over a prone body on the ground. Ignoring the sharp pain driving up from her knees, she groped for a gun among the dead man's clothes but he was unarmed, a deckhand taken down by the rebels. She leaped to her feet when Djari came around the bins.

He raised his gun. "They got our pilot. Come with me or we both die here today."

"I'm not going anywhere with you," she said, furious. Behind them, someone screamed. Another voice shouted something. The flashes of light through the air grew more sporadic. It had taken only seconds for the soldiers to contain the saboteurs.

He gripped her arm and shoved her toward the air lock.

Before she had a moment to consider a desperate lunge for his pistol, a hulking shape stepped between them. "That's our pilot," Captain Beryl said and twisted the weapon from Djari's hand before sending him to the floor with a chop of his powerful fist.

"They've cut the brakes on the climber," Nova said quickly. "It's going to blow when it gets here. I'm going to go after it."

Beryl handed her Djari's pistol. "What? How?"

Djari sat up, dazed by Beryl's blow. He felt for his boot and withdrew another gun. Beryl spun around faster than she thought someone of his size could move when he saw her eyes widen in surprise. He grabbed the front of her flight suit and tossed her behind a bin as if she were weightless. The first blast from Djari's pistol tore a hole into the container, the second one a hole into Captain Beryl's throat. The giant grunted in surprise as he lurched away, coughed a spray of blood, and collapsed.

Nova fled across the loading platform to the air lock. The

interior door was open but when she turned to reach for the controls she saw Djari racing after her.

"Stay away!" she shouted and aimed her gun.

He raised his arms toward her and let his pistol fall to the ground. "Don't leave me, Nova," he made a shambling half-turn to look back. Three of Beryl's men rushed toward them, looking primed to tear Djari's limbs from his body in frenzied retribution for their fallen leader. She saw bared teeth and balled fists and now-holstered weapons on these men who had no intention of capturing Djari alive.

Her jaw tightened until she heard her teeth grind. "Mitigate, Whiteside," she said and fired. Djari stopped and she shot him again.

She ran back to where he had fallen and knelt beside him. He turned his head briefly, squinting as if to fix her in his mind, and then he lay still.

"Alert the station that the climber is out of control and packed with explosives," she snapped at the soldiers. She saw Ancel beside the writhing shape of Captain Beryl, his hand clamped over the man's neck. "Tell them to open a secure channel to the cruiser out there. I want the Air Boss, and whatever damn engineer is still around to talk to me."

They gawked at her, considering her news. "On the fucking double!" she shouted, choking back tears of anger and regret and disappointment and all the other things that had no place in this moment.

She did not wait to see if they complied. She fumbled her way through the air lock sequence and entered the private cruiser moored there. Although the ship was a standard model used for small hops and a minimal passenger load, she recognized powerful modifications likely to be reckoned with in a firefight. Its design was familiar and, like all ships of this class, equipped with a neural interface. She placed the headset over the contact module at her temples to connect with navigation. Closing her eyes, she prayed to some of the local gods, just in case, but the system recognized her flight grade and allowed her control.

She released her grip on the air lock and punched out of the station's gravity well. The ship responded well to her tentative tests of its maneuverability and she soon felt it obey her mental commands without delay. "Tower, come in," she said. "Lieutenant Whiteside aboard rebel cruiser. Don't be shooting at me. Secure com link, please."

"Heard, Whiteside," came the reply which soon lost all formality. "Fill us in, Lieutenant, because what we just heard from the basement makes no sense. The climber is fine."

"Negative. Please just get me an engineer. And some backup out here would be nice, too. They've rewired something and the brakes are offline. I'm going to try to knock the climber off the ribbon. As soon as someone tells me how to do that."

"Got it. Good news bad news. It's past geosync so it won't fall to Bellac if it disengages. But that means we can't stop it."

"Heard, Tower. That's kinda the part that worried me." Nova steered the cruiser down along the tether to meet the arriving cargo pod. She reached for her seat restraint when she spun down the ship's gravity to avoid exerting its pull on the tether or the climber.

"Lieutenant," she heard another voice, this time the station commander.

"Yes, Colonel," she said. "How much time do we have?"

"None. The climber will reach the station in minutes. The lower levels are sealed. We are evacuating whom we can but we just don't have the pilots or the planes to get them all off."

"Respectfully, sir, this just isn't the sort of information I need right now."

There was a babble of voices and she winced when all of it sounded panicked and none of it intelligible. She slowed when the ship's instruments showed her the climber now approaching from below. She swung around it. This one had one open cargo platform stacked with supply containers like the ones she had seen on the station. It also carried one of the bulky, closed cargo pods designed to be transferred from the climber to a waiting ship, already processed and cleared by the Union base for forwarding shipment. "I'm there," she said. She rolled the cruiser and carefully matched the climber's speed, letting the ship calculate distance and velocity to its smallest increment.

"Lieut... Lieutenant?" a thin voice broke through her ear piece.

"The only one here," she said, focusing the ship's cameras onto the climber's grasp on the ridiculously thin tether.

"This is Sol Josel, station engineer. I've confirmed that our systems were... were tampered with. I won't be able to reset them quickly. That... that means... I mean."

"Look, Josel. Pull up your pants and tell me how to stop this thing. Can you do that? And I mean disengage it gently. Because if this thing blows it'll probably blow the tether, too." She looked over her displays. "I'll need them to shut down the upper shield network along the tether or I won't be able to get close."

"That... that would not be recommended. There is still some debris in orbit from the sabotage so it could possibly—"

"Colonel?" she said. "Getting a little short here."

"Shields are coming down, Whiteside," he replied. "Mr. Josel, if you please."

"What do I have that'll work?" Nova asked, having already sent the cruiser's specs up to the station.

"There is a forward utility laser. You should be able to reach the upper clamp guard with it."

"Heard." Nova directed the cruiser to hover to the left and engaged the laser's tracer to seek out the spot she needed. "Is that it?"

"No! That's the belt guide! You don't want to touch that."

"How about we pretend that I'm a pilot and you're the engineer. You can see what I see. And you can see my tracer, right?"

"Yes, to... to the left. That green hook-shape. If you can break that it'll loosen the clamps sufficiently. It'll take a lot of power."

"And then what'll happen?"

"The climber should drift away from the ribbon."

"When you say 'drift', do you mean spin off and crash into my ship?"

"Possibly."

"Going to invert, if you don't mind, Colonel." She moved her ship above the speeding climber and re-adjusted her gun.

"Clock's ticking, Whiteside."

"I can hear it from here," she said, never actually having heard the ticking of a clock. "Wait, this won't work. I can't get my tracer in there." She focused on her neural link, adjusting the ship's position again and again to achieve a different angle but each attempt brought another obstacle between her laser emitter and the target. "I can't get this. Is there any other way, short of making Bellac stop spinning?"

"Not without risking an explosion."

"We're already doing that." Nova cursed and looked around the narrow cockpit. "What about guns?" She reached up to pull a laser rifle from its holder on the bulkhead. "Got a Tan-Wat rail here."

She heard what might have been prayer over her earpiece. Resolutely, she locked the plane into a stationary position next to the climber and hurriedly dug through the storage bins near the ship's doors. It took little time to climb into a space suit and find a helmet that would connect to her neural interface. Knocking her gloves into place, she studied the external camera displays to send her mental commands to the navigator.

"Don't anyone breathe," she murmured to no one in particular as she moved the ship to align its external door with the top of the cargo pod. The systems faithfully continued to match the velocity of the climber toward the station. Satisfied that she was as close as she was going to get, she locked her helmet and engaged the air supply before opening the cruiser's small airlock chamber. An overhead compartment dropped a tether designed for exterior maintenance. She hooked the line to her harness, hooked up her gun as well, and opened the gate.

"Did I mention that I haven't done a spacewalk in... well, a while," she said. She peered out and down at the climber, certain that if she tried to look toward the distant planet she'd upchuck into her helmet. Somehow it didn't look quite so dizzying when viewed from inside the orbiter. Looking up toward the station approaching much too fast would probably have the same result.

"Easy, Lieutenant," the colonel's suddenly very gentle voice reached her. "You want no reverb at all. We have no idea how they packed the explosive."

She grasped the rail on the inside of the door and looked along the side of the ship. It was not one of the sleeker builds and she thought she could pull herself along without needing to touch the cargo container beneath her. She gripped the first of the planned handholds and pushed away from the door. She swung out, letting the inertia carry her forward and to the next point. "This suit is made for Caspians, by the way," she said, fumbling when the thick stub that accommodated a Caspian's additional thumb caught on something. It also explained the oversized boots that now bumped against the ship. "This gap looked a lot more narrow from inside the ship," she said when suddenly confronted by a whole lot of nothing between the cruiser and the climber's roller assembly.

"Lieutenant," Josel began, still sounding nervous.

"Call me Nova," she suggested. "Just in case we never meet again. Where from here?"

"There is a service rail. That red bar just ahead. You can use that to anchor yourself. You will have to push off from the ship. Softly!"

She braced a massive boot against the cruiser and shoved forward. For a breathless second she floated in space, secured only by the tether that bound her to the cruiser. The rail slipped into her hand as planned but her legs moved too far and bounced against another component of the climber which she didn't understand any better than the one she was about to shoot. She waited a moment for the climber, the cruiser, and herself to explode in a quiet storm of spare parts. She exhaled slowly when that didn't happen, willing her heart to return to a more reasonable pace.

"All right," she whispered. "I'm there."

"Whiteside," the colonel said. "You're doing a fine job."

"Always nice to hear, sir."

"If you can't disengage the climber, we're out of options and out of time. Get yourself out of there."

"I'm in place." She wedged her foot behind the rail and reached for her gun. "Is that it, Josel? Tell me it is because I'm about to shoot it."

"Yes. Yes, that's it. Your tracer is placed correctly. If that springs loose the rest will follow. Is… are we sure this a secure com line? Because this information… What? Oh."

"Can we all be quiet now?" Nova said. She steadied the gun and engaged the laser. Nothing happened for several seconds and then the color of the clamp guard changed and the unit twisted under the assault of her weapon. Briefly, she wondered if the gun carried a full charge.

"It's gone!" she cried. "Tore loose and slipped behind that white thingie."

"That *thingie* took a team of engineers five years to design," Josel said peevishly.

"Get out of there now, Whiteside," Colonel Thedris said. She thought she heard a smile in his voice. "If that didn't do it nothing else will."

Indeed, when she looked up she saw a space appear between the roller mount and the actual tether although a protective shield hid most of the attachment points. The elevator's graphene cable seemed to tilt away and she realized that the crawler itself was moving away from it. "Uh, I think it's loose but it's not moving anywhere fast."

Her comment was met only with silence.

"Hello? Could use a little help here. Something tells me that ranch is getting awfully close."

"Heard, Whiteside," the colonel said, now sounding all business. "Climber is not abandoning its trajectory. At this angle it will still hit the station."

"Hell, no," Nova muttered. She let the gun spin away and bent awkwardly to detach the clasp holding her line to the ship, her movements made clumsy by the six-fingered gloves. Gripping the service rail with one hand, she snapped the fastener onto it. A bead of sweat coursed its way into her eye and she blinked it away. The Caspian who usually wore this suit had set the controls far too high for her liking. "Why do they have fur, anyway?"

"Nova?"

"Busy. Call back later." Completely untethered now, she turned slowly and groped for the gently undulating line leading back to the cruiser. For a giddy instance she considered what might happen if she missed. Would they ever find her among the skyranch shrapnel before she ran out of air? Muttering about things she'd rather being doing right now, she pulled herself hand over hand to the ship and bumped awkwardly into the open air lock chamber.

"If you're attempting what I think you are…" Josel said.

"I am." She unsnapped the tether from the interior of the ship and clapped it onto the outside before punching the controls to pressurize the space. "I'm guessing a pull is better than a push right now."

"May the Gods find us all," he whispered.

She pulled off gloves and helmet and floated into the cabin to resume manual control of the ship. With infinite care, she rolled the ship, watching the main screen to see if the climber would pull away, or decide to swing into the tether itself. "Am I doing this right? I'm looking at all this upside down."

"Fall off a little more now," the colonel said. "The cable is taut. No sudden jerks."

She braced her feet against the cockpit ceiling and squeezed a little burst of power from the engines. Again, the elevator ribbon seemed to tilt before she understood that she, and her captive crawler, were veering away. Dimly, she became aware of the sound of several voices shouting with excitement and even one or two jubilant hoots. She wondered if that was the colonel hooting like that.

"Whiteside," she heard his voice only moments later. "That was some damn fine precision."

She smiled tiredly and boosted the ship again to tow the freefalling crawler to a safer distance. "Thank you, sir." She reached down to set a course away from the elevator and then turned to climb out of the pressure suit. "What do you want me to do with this thing?"

"Take it up to graveyard orbit. We're sending a salvage team to defuse it. Two of the rebels are still alive and are being questioned."

"What are their names?"

"Who? The rebels?"

Nova shook her head. "Never mind." She had seen Djari go down. And she had seen the look on the faces of Beryl's men. He would not be among the survivors. There was a tight, bothersome feeling somewhere in the center of her chest and she was unsure if it was grief or anger or a bit of both. Whatever it was, she wanted it gone.

How many had died here today? How many might have died if the rebels had succeeded? What battles were still raging at Siolet and the jumpsite? Did this have to happen?

"Sir, permission to join the engagement on Bellac?"

"Are you sure? You've done your share for the day."

"Positive. This ship is fully equipped."

"All right. Drop off the climber and be on your way. Make sure they know that you're on a cruiser." He paused for a moment. "Targon would be mad to deny your Hunter Class, I think."

TWELVE - EPILOGUE

Hours passed before Nova brought her ship down onto the landing apron of Skyranch Twelve and slipped into the clutch of the air lock pogs. Her eyes felt gritty for lack of sleep, her bruised ankle throbbed, she was hungry and wished for nothing more than a hot bath and a soft bed, neither of which was available on this station. Perhaps she could sneak into the therapy pool in the med station.

She had placed a call to Captain Dakad after finally leaving Bellac and heard that Beryl had survived the skirmish at the elevator hub. Apparently he was entirely made of leather and nanotubes or something. It didn't matter. What mattered was to finish this before his people caught her. And that meant staying out of their way for a little while longer.

She powered down and sat quietly for a moment, eyes closed. She wanted to cry. The head menders down on Bellac would approve of that. It was probably encouraged after shooting one's lover.

"Lieutenant?" a hesitant voice called out from behind her.

"Yes, yes, I'm awake. Welcome to Skyranch Twelve." She released the exit doors of the cruiser. The little cruiser was a fine piece of machinery and she had grown fond of it over these past few hours. Groaning, she pulled herself up, hid a gun behind the open flap of her flight suit, and stepped out of the plane.

The deck seemed abandoned when she and her passengers exited the lock. Banks of tranquil ceiling tiles illuminated the main concourse but the corridors leading to other parts of the orbiter were shadowed tunnels set to night shift power conservation.

"The lifts are this way," she said.

They headed to the left and she was not surprised when she found their way barred by a security detail. Not just any, of course, but Beryl's squad. She turned to see more of them step up from behind. They stood silently and looked about as menacing as she had ever seen them.

Sergeant Rafe stepped forward, gun in hand although not quite aimed at her. He glowered at her and then at the five people that had traveled with her from Bellac. Slowly, recognition seemed to come to him.

"Sergeant," Nova said politely. "You may remember some of these good folks." She turned to the huddle of pale-faced visitors who were unable to take their eyes from the soldiers' guns. "You know Doctor Soren, of course. You'll recall meeting Doctor Luca Vidarron. And here is Sergeant Daphine Hayden, Specialist Abrana, and Specialist Gosen."

"What is this?" Rafe growled.

"They've come to visit with the colonel. Isn't that nice of them?"

"Giving you a choice, Whiteside. You can turn around and get off this station with these people, never to return, or you're coming below with us. What's it going to be?"

"Below? Oh, you mean down where you've got all that *mince* stashed?"

"Somewhere there, yeah. I was thinking you'll boil down into a fine soup for the grow rings, like the rest of the garbage."

Lights came on in the corridor spaces, removing every

last shadow with its unwavering glare. Beryl's men looked around themselves when armed soldiers and some of the station's pilots moved in to surround the group, weapons ready.

From the direction of the lifts came a curious collection of mechanics, two pilots, and several of the surviving workers from the loading dock. Nova recognized the nervous Bellac she had tackled in the stairwell and gave him a glad smile. Captain Dakad hovered protectively near them but his eyes were on Rafe and his expression seemed grimmer than usual.

Colonel Thedris stepped forward. "Lieutenant Whiteside, I'm pleased to see you in one piece, I have to say."

"Thank you, sir." She nodded to Dakad. "Is the shipping level still sealed off, Captain?"

"It is," he replied. "Except for the bomb squad and medics no one's been down there."

Rafe grunted something and shifted his gun. Immediately, several security personnel moved forward and disarmed him and his companions.

"Colonel, these people, along with those Captain Dakad assembled, will offer a deposition in support of my charges. You will find a number of blue bins labeled as food stuffs and destined for Magra on the docks. Each of those bins was cleared for customs by Captain Beryl and his men under the direct guidance of Major Trakkas. The bins contain *mince* in various forms, brought into Shon Gat by caravan and from there to the elevator depot."

"Trakkas? That's quite the accusation, Lieutenant."

"The deck hands that survived will corroborate, as will the crew members from Rim Station where similar smuggling took place. Captain Beryl used a systematic method of intimidation and blackmail to gain cooperation from those not directly involved. Doctors Soren and Vidarron are able to share enough information for you to investigate patient files showing evidence of physical assaults and at least one murder. These things probably also happened down at the

Shon Gat base."

The colonel turned slowly to look over several of Beryl's people. Rafe took a threatening step toward Nova and was restrained at once. "He took a bullet for you, bitch."

She regarded him coldly. "He was doing his job," she said. "And now I'm doing mine." She turned back to the colonel. "Their smuggling operation caught the attention of the Shri-Lan who inserted their own people among ours, including Nathon Djari. That allowed them to hide explosive materials in the boxes of *mince* as well as the climber that I was able to disengage."

"What?" Rafe shouted, outrage and disbelief clear on his face.

"I believe that the siege at Shon Gat was staged to let us assume that the militants had all been expelled from the town. Once they were gone along with any immediate threat of terrorism, the rebels were free to work out the sabotage." She raised her chin toward Rafe. "Aided by our own people. As you probably guessed, today's attack on Siolet and the jumpsite was yet another diversion to scatter our forces and give the Shri-Lan agents time to position the explosives around the elevator hub and the lower level."

The colonel looked over the small crowd gathered here and saw several people nodding while others just threw fearful glances at the disarmed guards. "How long has this been going on?" he said to Rafe.

The men stared back at him, silent.

The colonel turned back to Nova. "And Major Trakkas was aware of all this?"

"Yessir, although I don't know if he was leading these men or if he was simply a... beneficiary."

"How did you find all this?"

"By accident," she said. "But I will also admit that I should have realized much sooner that something... unusual was going on down at the docks. But—"

"That'll do, Lieutenant," the colonel said, ready to get over the shock of this revelation. "We will take this from here. Major Eagan, have these men taken away and place a watch on Captain Beryl's hospital room. Contact Shon Gat and make the appropriate arrangement for Major Trakkas and the ground crew. Have all shipping records for the past year encrypted and delivered up here." He gestured to the others. "Each of you will make an individual statement with full disclosure. You would not be here if you weren't prepared to do so, am I correct?"

There were hesitant nods all around, more emphatic once Beryl's men had been led from the concourse.

He instructed his aide to make cabins available to the arrivals from Bellac before waving Nova aside. She walked with him to the impressive observation window looking out over the grow rings. There was a narrow bench there but she knew that if she sat down now it would be impossible to get up again.

"You're looking a little peaked, Whiteside," Thedris said with a smile.

"Been a long day, sir."

He clasped his hands behind his back. "You took risks, Lieutenant."

"Yes, sir. I have regrets. I allowed myself to be intimidated by these men. I'm not proud of that. I should have—"

He waved that aside. "Learn from it, Whiteside, and move on. The only thing you need to analyze right now are your odds of making Hunter Class. Which are pretty damn good, from what I've seen."

"You'll approve the application, then?"

"I'm signing off on those remaining hours in the morning. You can leave for Targon on the next transport."

She sighed deeply. "I won't let you down, sir." Her eyes wandered to the cruiser visible through the window. "I'm wondering if I could... I mean, could I... um, take that ship? Next transport isn't for weeks."

He looked outside. "Spoils of war, Lieutenant? Promise you'll wait a few days to get into top shape before you go?"

"Promise. Can I take Lieutenant Rolyn with me as wingman?"

He nodded. "If Dakad concurs."

"Can I—"

He laughed. "Go to bed, Whiteside. That's an order."

ABOUT THE AUTHOR

Chris Reher is a first generation Canadian currently and out of necessity residing on planet Earth (which, in the general and interplanetary scheme of things, could *really* use a catchier name. Imagine heading past Proxima Centauri and someone asks you whence you came and you tell them "dirt". All theological implications aside, that just won't do.)

When not finding ways to defy the laws of physics or torture her subjects or entice them with inter-species hanky-panky, she designs web sites or writes about designing web sites. She enjoys long walks on the beach or, given the local beach shortage, writes about beaches far beyond Proxima Centauri.

www.chrisreher.com

Sky Hunter
The Catalyst
Only Human
Rebel Alliances
Delphi Promised

Quantum Tangle
Terminus Shift
Entropy's End